I0670349

BIRTHDAY
by Jana Egle

Translated by Uldis Balodis

Curated by Kaija Straumanis as part of the 2025 Translator Triptych

OPEN LETTER
LITERARY TRANSLATIONS FROM THE UNIVERSITY OF ROCHESTER

Originally published as *Dzimšanas diena* by Latvijas mēdiji, 2020
Copyright © Jana Egle, 2020
Translation copyright © Uldis Balodis, 2025

First edition, 2025
All rights reserved.

Library of Congress Cataloging-in-Publication data: Available.
ISBN (pb): 978-1-960385-15-4 | ISBN (ebook): 978-1-960385-22-2

This project is supported in part by an award from the National Endowment for the Arts.

This project is also made possible by the New York State Council on the Arts with the support of the Office of the Governor and the New York State Legislature.

Cover design by Jenny Volvovski

Published by Open Letter at the University of Rochester
Morey Hall 303, Rochester, NY 14627
www.openletterbooks.org

Printed on permanent/durable acid-free paper in Canada

BIRTHDAY

CONTENTS

LITTLE DACE AND THE TWINS

"Dace! Dace!"

Dace wakes up slowly. Square patches of sunlight shimmer through the window and scatter across the floor. She crawls out of bed and stands up, her bare feet resting on the warm floorboards painted brown. Shadows have taken two round bites out of one of the sunlit patches and Dace realizes that someone is calling her. As expected, through the window she can see one reddish and one bright-white head of hair. Gunārs and Elmārs, the twins from the other end of the house. Dace lives on this end with her mom, dad, granny, and gramps. But on the other end—Gunārs and Elmārs with their mom and dad. The twins are six years old, which is almost the same as Dace, since she's turning six tomorrow. The twins' dad is almost always drunk, but their mom is very pretty, as long as she's not also drunk. But when she is, she's as messy as a hog eating slop, as Dace's gramps says. The twins' dad always manages to stay upright no matter how much he drinks and when pretty Elvīra is on the sauce, he knocks her about like an old sack of rags.

9

Late last night the twins' parents fought again. The thuds and swearing coming from the other side of the wall didn't stop even when it was time for Dace to go to bed. So they'll sleep until afternoon. The boys can do whatever they want now. Dace is jealous, she never gets to do whatever she wants. Her life is so gray and dull.

"Hey, Dace!" red-haired Gunārs doesn't let up. "C'mere! I wanna show you somethin'!"

Dace hangs out the window and the brothers let go of the windowsill and tumble off the side of the house.

"What do you got?" Elmārs tugs angrily at his brother's shirt. "Show me first!"

Gunārs just keeps giggling, covering his mouth with his hand.

"Are you gonna come out?" he winks at Dace. Dace can't get out just like that. First, she has to walk through the living room and then the kitchen. Somebody—either Granny or Gramps—is definitely going to be there. She'll have to wash her face, brush her hair, and eat breakfast right away.

"Just wait a sec, okay? I'll . . . just a sec," Dace whispers loudly to the brothers and dashes over to the huge wardrobe in the corner of the room.

The key is a little too high to grab, but the girl has no shortage of guts, and after a little bit of effort she has the creaking wooden doors open.

"Aughh!" Dace screams and slams the doors shut again. Her mom's mink had been staring up at her from the corner of the bottom shelf—a ghastly creature with empty hollows for eyes and a toothless mouth frozen in a wicked grin. Dace is terribly afraid of it, but her clothes are sitting right above that thing in the wardrobe. With one eye closed—the one facing the mink—she carefully opens the wardrobe again and, clutching the first pieces of clothing in reach, slams the doors shut and locks them. The beast doesn't even get a chance to squeak. Fully dressed now, she pushes the chair over to the window, struggles up onto the windowsill, and dangles her legs outside. The brothers are poking around with sticks underneath the bushes and are quietly muttering something.

"There's a really huge caterpillar down here," Elmārs announces enthusiastically as soon as he notices Dace. "Hey, are you gonna jump down?" he calls out with surprise.

"Uh-huh," the girl answers hesitantly.

Gunārs also quits poking the caterpillar and—just as excited as his brother—waits for Dace to jump.

"We'll catch you," they yell and the brothers stretch out their arms to grab her, disheveled and flushed with jitters.

Something catches and rips loudly. Her support squad scatter in opposite directions and Dace tumbles down into the dusty bushes, right onto her face. While Gunārs and Elmārs are bent over laughing, Dace touches the back of her dress—seems like everything's okay, but what ripped?

"Stop laughing and look for what ripped back there," she stands up and mutters angrily. The brothers walk around Dace, each from his own direction, and then circle her again, and—fully convinced—announce in unison:

"It looks fine!"

"Great, now show me what you've got!" Elmārs comes around first and pokes his brother in the stomach. Gunārs has some kind of small package tucked under his shirt and proudly pulls it out. A wrinkled newspaper. None of them knows how to read yet and Dace even starts getting a little angry, but Gunārs starts unwrapping something from it. A tin. Shiny, red, and covered in print. At the store they sell halva in tins like this, or those tiny, colorful Montpensier fruit drops, which are usually stuck together in a big, solid lump.

"Can you guess what's inside?" Gunārs asks, clearly lording his knowledge over them. "Halva! Candy! A spider! Kopecks!" Dace and Elmārs scream over each other, but each time Gunārs just shakes his head. "Nails! Gooseberries! Come on, stop! How are we supposed to guess! Colored wires! Buttons!"

Gunārs keeps shaking his head and Dace and Elmārs are all out of ideas. Pausing for dramatic effect, Gunārs finally announces:

"I shit in it!" He twists the lid off the tin and, yes, there really is a turd in there.

Elmārs immediately flaps his hands along his sides and wipes them on his shirt as if he had touched the turd himself, while Dace feels a simultaneous sense of disgust and wonder. She never says words like that, mom and dad don't let her, so that's why Dace only says "poop," but "shit" sounds so confident and proud that despite the stench and the wish to flap her hands just like Elmārs, she declares—just as confidently as Gunārs:

"Wow, you shit in there!"

All three of them stare at the turd for a moment. Gunārs wistfully, but Elmārs and Dace grimacing a bit.

"What are you gonna do with it?" Dace asks, interrupting the thoughtful silence.

"Let's put the tin on the path by the pharmacy and watch from the bushes. Somebody will think it has candy in it, but instead find a turd inside!"

Gunārs laughs loudly and heartily. Elmārs and Dace think that somebody will definitely freak out and scream seeing the turd in the tin, and they laugh along with Gunārs. It'll be an amazing joke!

The pharmacy is just behind Uncle Jāzeps and Aunt Zigrīda's house. You have to walk through the berry bushes, along the back of the barn, past the neighbors' well, and then straight to the pharmacy. The trip takes them down the narrow path that winds through the thicket of mugwort, Gunārs in front holding the tin, followed by Dace, and Elmārs dragging behind.

"I want a drink," Elmārs whines upon seeing the well. "Well, go get one then." Gunārs looks back.

"I don't know how . . ."

Elmārs has always been weaker and more timid than his half-an-hour-older brother.

"Okay, then hold this," Gunārs thrusts the tin at him and Elmārs obediently takes it with the fingertips of both hands. The boy's nose twists completely sideways, and his eyebrows dart up, driving three fine, deep clefts into his well-tanned forehead.

Gunārs grabs resolutely for the well's crank. It's not easy, but the bucket slowly descends, deeper and deeper, banging and rattling along the well's sides.

"Hey, how far is the water?" the little muscleman can't let go of the crank to look down and so asks the others.

13

The reflections of two bright little heads appear in the well's black waters, along with two outstretched hands no longer able to hold onto the turd tin; it slips and falls with a loud crash right into the bucket, which sits just above the water. The impact knocks off the tin's lid and all of Gunārs's efforts from the morning splatter all over the water bucket.

"Oh, you dummy, you're a real ding-dong!" Gunārs lets go of the crank, and looks into the well, cursing at his brother. The words echo wonderfully in the well.

"Oooo! Dinnng-donnng! Bow, wow, wow! Shit! Shit! Aughhh! Kalimbamba!" all three rascals shout over each other into the dark well, swinging their disheveled heads, listening to the echoes. Meanwhile, the counterbalance is slowly bringing the bucket back up, filled with its new treasures.

"What now?" Dace asks Gunārs.

"We've got to rinse it out," the red-haired boy says wisely and grabs for the crank again. "Give me a hand, let's get the bucket back down, fill it with water, then pull it back up and wash it. We can't just leave it."

The three of them grab onto the crank and force the bucket back down. Dace is the first to hear that something isn't right. Somebody is coming down the path behind the barn and the lilac bushes, their steps scraping ominously on the dry grass. She lets go of the crank and dashes into the mugwort, Elmārs right behind her, but Gunārs takes a second too long and then Uncle Jāzeps—the owner of the house and well—appears around the corner of the barn. Gunārs barely manages to slip into the underbrush along the path, but it looks like Uncle Jāzeps spotted his ginger head of hair. Then the hook complete with bucket slowly rises up out of the well.

Crouching like baby swallows behind the wood pile in Dace's parents' shed, the three of them sit quietly for a moment—six smudged and skinned knees in a row—listening to Uncle Jāzeps's bellowing, which is joined a moment later by the tinkling of Aunt Zigrīda's little voice, which also turns very quickly into piercing shrieks. The sounds of buckets clanging, water splashing, and colorful swear words force their way into the shed through the gaps in the boards. It seems like the neighbors won't be offering them all the apples they can eat this summer.

A moment later the noise has stopped.

"I'm hungry," Elmārs whispers.

"I'm hungry, I'm thirsty," Gunārs mocks him, but feels the same gurgle in his tummy. And Dace hasn't eaten at all yet today.

Grandma has a cookhouse at the far end of the stables, which she uses to make food for the farm animals. Every morning there is a pot of cooked turnips on the stove for the pigs, and bread for the calves sitting in stacks on the shelf, its dark crust often having separated from the rest of the loaf. These turnips and bread were tastier than all the beet soups and meatballs in the world, so the hungry trio knew right away where to go.

The door of the cookhouse is shut. Locked. That's a real surprise, usually it's open—day or night. But Dace and Gunārs aren't giving up. There's a door on the other side of the cookhouse too. It's higher and always locked, but there's a gap underneath it. Dace has grabbed turnips and bread crusts out from under there when one of the grown-ups has been working in the kitchen—the twins aren't allowed to go in there at all.

They go around and get on their hands and knees, butts in the air, and peer in through the gap under the cookhouse door.

15

Not a soul to be seen, but instead of the pot of turnips, there's some kind of device warming on the stove—a big jug with a series of tubes twisting into little coils and spirals, everything hissing and steaming, and all the while water drips from the spout. Somebody must have forgotten to shut it off. While the two of them stare at all of this mouths agape, Elmārs has snuck up behind them and lets out a roaring laugh.

"Dace, I can see your butt! Hey, bare butt, bare butt!"

Dace jumps to her feet and reaches behind her back. How could it be, it was impossible. She'd even risked an attack from that hideous, toothless mink when she'd yanked those pants out of the wardrobe, and had absolutely, for certain pulled them up all the way. But feeling her behind it becomes suddenly clear what the tearing sound had been when she'd jumped out the window. Her pants are torn all the way to the waist band, hanging completely open to expose one of her butt cheeks. There is nothing to do but go home and look for a different pair . . . Dace sighs, but what can she do. And, after all, she's hungry.

When they go back around behind the stables, pretty Elvīra—who doesn't look all that pretty today—is running across the field with her black, disheveled hair like a witch's, and loudly screaming:

"Elmārs! Gunārs!"

The twins spin around and try to disappear behind the stables, but Elvīra is as angry as she is sharp-eyed and quick. In one fell swoop, she grabs both boys, who by now are kicking and screaming. But Elvīra holds them fast like a hawk in her long, stiff fingers, and drags the two young chicks inside the house.

Dace waits for a minute longer as the howling whirlwind disappears with them behind their door, and then goes home. Granny and Gramps are bustling around the kitchen and seem somehow nervous and in a hurry. Granny is standing by the sink, scrubbing bottles with a brush, then rinsing them and arranging them in a row on the table, which is covered in newspaper. Gramps is rummaging around the junk drawer and pulling out corks for the bottles, one by one. When Dace walks in, they seem startled and stare at her with unconcealed surprise.

"What? Huh?" Granny stutters in surprise.

"You said she was asleep!" Gramps mutters angrily.

To take some of the attention off of her, Dace puts her hands on her hips, fixes her eyebrows in an angry expression, and launches a counterattack.

"You're up to some sort of mischief here, but meanwhile there's a real sabantuy going on in your cookhouse!

Dace didn't know what a sabantuy was, but Mom would use it when something had really gone off the rails, and Dace felt that this was just the right time.

"What's in the cookhouse?!" Gramps asks Dace, while staring with bulging eyes at Granny.

"It's all huffing and puffing though a bunch of tubes and there's water dripping!" Dace shoots back.

Granny glances at Gramps, Gramps at Granny, and in a huff Granny says:

"I told you we shouldn't do it during the day."

Gramps puffs out his chest and says:

"So I'm supposed to keep the girl in check?"

But Dace strides proudly between them and heads to her room for some new pants.

While she's standing by the wardrobe trying to summon up enough courage to fling open the door to reveal the lair of that hideous mink, Granny walks in holding a comb.

"You need to comb your hair, a girl needs to look pretty, tidy, and sweet."

Granny grabs her head, and Dace puffs out her cheeks to get through the methodical plucking, but thinks to herself that pretty doesn't always equal sweet. Elvīra is pretty but pointy as a thorn and with a tongue as sharp as barbed wire. Dace's mom on the other hand is sweet and tidy, but not particularly pretty . . . Her whole head hurts, just as it always does when the comb is in Granny's hands, and Dace not only puffs out her cheeks, but clenches her eyes shut so tightly that she sees spinning, multi-colored rings. Suddenly there's a commotion next door; Elvīra must have dragged the twins to their room. Elvīra is screaming:

"Hooligans! Don't you have any shame?! You shat in Uncle Jāzeps's well, you went and took a shit in his well! And then lied about it! You should be put on a rocket and shot to Mars, just so there's some peace and quiet around here!"

Thuds, bumps, and tremors can be heard through the wall. One of them is wailing, the other one yells:

"That doesn't even hurt!"

Another thud.

"It doesn't hurt, see!"

Dace's head doesn't hurt anymore. She feels sorry for Gunārs and Elmārs and is a tiny bit afraid they'll tell that she'd been there too.

It all ends with someone yelling, "You little shits are staying in your room today!" The throttling on the other side of the wall has ended. Right at that moment Granny is putting a ribbon around one of her curly locks; she ties it into a bow and says:

"Come along now, you need to eat something."

"Wait, lemme think."

Granny chuckles and walks toward the kitchen. Dace is still afraid of the mink, but isn't she a brave girl? After the horrors the brothers next door had to experience, all she needs to do is not be afraid of one little animal. The girl flings open the wardrobe doors quick as can be and, grabbing some pants, slams them shut again.

Without the twins, the day is sad and boring. Wandering around the house, Dace goes up to the boys' window twice and both times taps cautiously on the pane with a stick. The first time, nothing happens; they must have cried themselves to sleep, she thinks. The second time, two heads—one red-haired, one bright white—pop up behind the glass. But the windows stays closed.

"We're not allowed to open it!" they call out in unison, and Dace can just barely make out what they're saying.

Gunārs presses his cheek right up to the windowpane while rolling his eyes and twisting his head, his face and nose are flat and white, it looks so hideous that Dace bursts out laughing again. Then Elmārs also shoves his nose and lips against the glass, sticks out his tongue, and starts fooling around. Dace is laughing so hard that the boys can't help it either, and all three of them have their mouths gaping as wide as the frogs in the pond behind the house. But in the next instant the brothers glance nervously over their shoulders, quickly scramble away, and the window sits empty and expressionless again, reflecting just a few little, lazy, white clouds idling high in the sky.

Dace decides to walk to the store. The brothers won't be allowed outside, but she can go see the wonderful doll sitting on the shelf at the store. Dace has been begging and pleading for at least two weeks for Mom and Dad to buy it for her. But they don't even turn their heads when she grabs them by the hand and says: "Come on, Mom, come and look at what a pretty doll she is, come on, just look!" They must think it's much more interesting to watch the clerk slice butter or sausage and then weigh and wrap it in paper, or use a scoop to pour sugar into a paper bag, or fish around for herring in the big, shiny metal barrel. Meanwhile, the doll sits with its long dress the color of egg yolks, vibrant, cornflower-blue eyes, golden hair, and little white shoes. Unable to penetrate her parents' wall of indifference, Dace runs to the store every day to embrace the unreachable, untouchable beauty with her eyes. But today she'll summon up her strength and ask the clerk to let her hold the doll for just a moment. Dace runs into the store out of breath, there's only some strange lady in line in front of her, the clerk will be free in a second, and then . . . And then Dace sees that the shelf is empty, and the doll is gone . . . Dace's little mouth hangs half open in an unasked question, and her eyes burn with tears. It's sad, so very sad that Dace, her face flushed from crying, walks home and doesn't talk to anyone for the rest of the day. Only in the evening when Mom finally gets home from work and choir practice, and comes in to see what her little sweetheart is up to, does Dace snuggle up close to her and quietly confess what's weighing on her:

"Mommy, that pretty doll wasn't at the store anymore . . ."

Hot, pained tears flow as she starts crying again. Her mom presses her warm lips against Dace's forehead.

"It's bedtime, sweetie. At night our sorrows can look huge and invincible, but by morning they've gotten so tiny that sometimes they disappear altogether."

But none of that helps Dace at all. Her heart aches, and the immense longing for the boundlessly beautiful doll can't be tamped down by Mom's wisdom.

When Dace is in bed and her tears have dried, she hears her dad getting home too. Gramps tells him proudly that he'd knocked out a dozen bottles, if you don't count the piss left over at the end. "How awful," Dace thinks, "what a stinky day—shit in the morning and piss at night." But now sleep envelops her, so sweet, fuzzy, and soft. She still hears Mom and Granny watching a concert on the TV in the living room. While the announcer talks, Granny says:

"Imagine, Elvīra's boys crapped in Jāzeps's well today."

Mom inhales sharply.

"What? Crapped in it? How's that even possible? No, those twins are nuts and they'll stay nuts. We got so lucky with ours, Dace would never do something like that."

Granny laughs and says:

"But boy did they get it. The whole house shook while Elvīra was dealing with them."

After a moment of silence, they turn their attention to the soloist's pretty dress, and Granny announces sagely:

21

"Margarita Vilcāne has such strangely long arms, those flowing sleeves suit her . . ."

And then Dace drifts off completely to a dreamland where Gramps is knocking out a dozen bottles in the yard, a magically beautiful doll with terribly long arms dances, its bright yellow sleeves fluttering, undulating with frilly ruffles, dancing, getting further and further away until it disappears into a warm, white light, singing among sparse clouds. A little later, when Dace wakes up to pee, Gramps and Dad are sitting in the kitchen—red-faced and with sleeves rolled up—both humming the melody of Gramps's favorite song, "Praying softly, my song echoes in the quiet night . . ."

Dace also likes the song, but she knows that Gramps won't sing for long and will soon start sniffling, and by the end of the verse Dad will be singing alone again in his thin, trembling voice, "Come comfort meeee!"

Dace crawls back into bed and is lulled by all of tonight's songs, an instant later falling into a gentle but deep, dreamless slumber.

The next morning squeezes its way through the window with a cascade of warm sun beams, and a heavenly aroma flows in from the direction of the kitchen. It smells like Granny's unbeatable specialty—fritters.

They are cooked in oil, white, soft, and fluffy on the inside with a crunchy, brown crust on the outside. Dace jumps happily out of bed and runs to the fritters in her nightshirt. Scurrying through the living room, she dashes into the kitchen and clutches Granny around the waist.

"Granny, fritters!"

Granny, covered in flour, is rolling the stiff, brown parchment paper with a rolling pin. Dace knows that there is sugar crackling between the two layers of paper—when Granny rolls it out, it'll become powdered sugar. But right there on the table is a big bowl painted with cherries and apples, already full of the round brown fritters. Granny smiles, looks at Dace, and says:

"How did you manage to run through that room so fast? Happy birthday, Dace!" And she leans down to give the girl a kiss on a cheek still ruddy from sleep.

"It's my birthday!" Dace squeals happily.

"Get dressed, I'll comb your hair, Mom put your pretty dress out for you. But don't rush through the living room." Granny gives her a pointed look while rolling the dough.

Dace doesn't catch her drift and heads off to get dressed so she can get to eating sooner. She walks into the living room, and there! There, sitting on the table, is the doll! With her cornflower blue eyes and her little white shoes! Dace shrieks, she grabs the doll, and hugs her tightly, as tightly as she can. Tears flow onto the golden hair and silken dress, but Dace is happy. Granny is looking through door, laughing, and calls out:

"What are you blubbering about? It's time to get ready for the party."

Dace changes quickly into her new blue dress with the little white pompoms on the sleeves, puts on some white ankle-socks, also with little pompoms, and is all ready for her birthday morning fritters.

Clutching the doll, Dace takes everything down to breakfast. Granny combs and ties her ponytail again—this time with a white ribbon. But just as the birthday girl is ready to eat, there's a knock on the door. Dace runs to open it herself, and there they are—Gunārs, Elmārs, and their mom—pretty, made-up, and perfumed. The twins too—their hair slicked back, faces washed, and wearing white shirts. Stepping across the threshold, the three of them—prompted by Elvīra—start singing "Happy birthday." The boys are singing unwillingly and clumsily, Elvīra enthusiastically, poking whichever one stops singing or is going too slow, but Dace is looking at the boys' hands. Elmārs has a bunch of flowers picked from the garden, the bitter smell of marigolds and heady scent of sweet peas breaks through the enticing aroma of the fritters. Gunārs, however, is holding a tin of candies tied with a ribbon. Dace knows this orange tin well, it usually contains her favorite kind of candy—Milk Drops. But this time there's a touch of anxiety worming its way through Dace's stomach, and she isn't at all sure that she wants to open this present.

THE DEBT

It's raining outside. The drops striking the windowsill create a rhythmic beat that sounds like light jazz. Every so often, a white flash illuminates the distant horizon, followed by a crash a few seconds later that echoes across the sky. This is the first spring thunderstorm; tomorrow they'll be able to sit outside.

Dita is standing at the window in her home, an opened letter in her hands, waiting for Niks to drive up with their two smallest children. That morning they'd gone to Niks's mother's place to get some potatoes—they didn't have any of their own left. His mother probably had some "men's work" sitting around for Niks to do, but he should be home at any moment. Outside the rain is hacking away at the linden leaves and brutally crushing silken petals as it pushes the red tulips and blue hyacinths level with the ground. It's a nice place to live. Dita likes looking after their home. Planning, caring, tending, planting—doing all of it calmly and with gratitude. And waiting for the flowers and fruit to bloom. But this year, somehow, she's tired; maybe the winter was a bit too long and cold.

The letter reads—if you don't start paying your debt in a month's time, all of your property at your declared residence will be seized. She puts her hands on her lower abdomen and gently strokes it saying: "Don't worry, everything will be okay. Mommy is a little worried, but you're safe. I love you very much and am waiting for you. And your brothers and sisters are waiting for you too. We have a big house and a beautiful yard with swings and a slide, you'll be so happy here."

Dita knows that she needs to think happy thoughts while pregnant; she's going to have her sixth child. The littlest ones—four-year-old Dārta and six-year-old Silvestrs—were thrilled at the news and immediately got into an argument—Dārta wants a sister, but Silvestrs wants a brother. The older children were surprised and just smiled, but Niks's expression didn't change at all. It was at their lunch together on Easter Sunday when Dita—so nervous that she felt like her cheeks were on fire—told all of them at once about their little miracle. Niks clapped his palm against the oak table a few times and didn't say a word. In the last six weeks they hadn't talked about it at all. Dita remembers how angry he'd been when Marts—their third child—had announced his presence. "Dita, children have to be supported and provided for until they're at least eighteen! Fully supported, you understand?" But now Niks gets along with thirteen-year-old Marts the best of all. And Marts is a lot like his father. When Silvestrs and Dārta came into the world, one after another, Niks barely protested at all. This time he didn't say a thing. He must have understood that there's no sense wasting words.

Dita's cat—young, little, calico Minna—is sitting on the windowsill. She's blinking her eyes, purring quietly, and watching drops of water slide down the glass. Minna's stomach is really fat. Dita feels the subtle, maternal bond that connects them. But Minna doesn't yet know the gentleness and joy that newborns can bring; this is her first time. Maybe she'll get all six in one go.

Dita turns away from the window and listens; the washing machine seems to be silent now. She takes the clean, wet clothes out of the drum and carries them over to the empty room on the other side of the house to hang them up. They don't even have a floor laid down yet, just thick crossbeams with sawdust poured in between. She needs to move carefully so she doesn't trip. Dita likes the smell of this room—wood pulp with a hint of apples. In the fall, they store the winter apples here until they're all eaten, but their scent seems to soak into the sawdust and doesn't disappear until the spring. Dita hangs the laundry on the lines stretching across the room, then goes back and puts the next load of laundry into the machine. She'll wash Niks's work clothes last. He always gets oil and rust on himself at the auto shop; she has to run the heavy-duty cycle and use a stronger detergent. There's a little bit of time right now, she'll start the soup later; maybe Niks and the little ones will have eaten at mom's, but the older kids will have had lunch at school. And there aren't any potatoes yet either. Rita thinks she should call Niks so he can make a quick detour and grab Marts, Roberts, and Asnate on the way, but she doesn't for some reason and instead starts washing the floors. There are many rooms, and this job is easier to get done if no one else is home.

When the car drives up, everything is clean and tidy. Niks and the younger kids come in through the door just as she is taking the next load of laundry out of the machine, piling it into a large, blue plastic bin, and dragging it off again to the other end of the house. Niks looks on but doesn't help Dita carry any of it. She doesn't have to go far, but Dita still feels annoyed. While she is hanging the damp clothes on the line, she hears the lid of the pot clank in the kitchen. Someone must be trying to find something to eat. Then the door opens and Niks comes in holding the letter. Dita had left it on the kitchen table.

"It's time to figure out what we're going to do, and we have to start making payments," he says.

"Yes," Dita answers as she continues dealing with the laundry. She takes a pillowcase, shakes it out with both hands so it snaps, and then carefully smooths it out with her hands and puts it over the stretched line. Then she takes another pillowcase, then a towel, and then Dārta's little sheet. She shakes out each one, puts it over the line, smooths it out with her hands. Niks stands there for a moment and then walks back toward the kitchen. Dita feels a sharp twinge in her lower abdomen, but she knows that can happen sometimes in pregnancy and doesn't worry about it.

Dita doesn't know if she still loves Niks. Sometimes she thinks about how she's never again going to feel that little tickle in her solar plexus on her way to a date. She'll never again get to anticipate the brush of lips she doesn't yet know. Dita closes her eyes and almost feels the physical sensation of a long, deep kiss, her tongue sliding through another man's lips. Niks has been apathetic for a long time, maybe once every two weeks he'll run his hands across her breasts in a perfunctory manner

28

while they're still covered by her nightie and then, pulling it up a bit, will enter her passionlessly, and too soon, and then eventually reach his own climax. And it's been forever since he's asked her if it was good. Maybe Niks has someone else. Dita repeats this thought to herself several times and tries to understand what she feels. Does it hurt or upset her? Would she want him to leave? Maybe it would easier, simpler, and better for her to be alone? Roberts is already seventeen, and when the little one is born he'll be eighteen. And by the time he's grown, they'll be old. Maybe she won't care about anything then. Maybe she already doesn't. Dita never has the time to stop and think, to understand what she really feels about Niks. Or maybe she's just trying to convince herself that she doesn't have the time, so she doesn't have to face a truth she doesn't yet know. And once she does, what will she do then?

She needs to go make the soup. Niks didn't pick up the older kids on the way. It's already afternoon, they'll be hungry. Minna meows somewhere in the corner; her meow sounds drawn out and scared. Dita walks over and finds the cat's worn blanket in the basket. A rosy fluid has stained the cloth and the cat's little, calico body is already shaking from contractions.

"Minna, sweetie, everything's okay, don't worry," Dita whispers, stroking the cat's head and side.

The little creature snuggles up to her hand, purring and growling at the same time. Her front paws are kneading empty air, her eyes are wide from fright, but the cat instinctively knows what to do—she doesn't need a midwife or any help.

Dita walks out of the room and closes the door firmly behind her. For now, she won't tell the little ones, so the cat can deal with her new arrivals in peace. Dita feels a twinge in her stomach again. Maybe next time she should call the doctor, the spasms are coming more often than with the others. But, of course, she's not getting any younger. Her body has probably gotten tired from her many pregnancies . . .

"Mom, Silvestrs won't give me back my doll!"

Dārta runs up and clings to her leg, furiously and with crystal clarity enunciating her brother's name. She learned to pronounce "r" only last week and so is especially emphatic whenever she has an opportunity to show off her new ability. Dārta's hair smells like Dita's mother-in-law's house—the stale, dusty drapery of the curtains, Corvalol, and vanilla.

Dita feels sick and pushes her daughter away. Silvestrs is skipping around the room, holding the doll by its leg, and spinning it over his head. Dārta begins to pout and darts after her brother, but all her attempts to get back her property are in vain—the boy is taller and quicker than her, and he likes to tease his sister.

"Silvestrs, stop bothering your sister!" Dita yells, but by then Dārta has started to cry, and no one hears what Mom is saying anymore. Niks comes in, snatches the doll out of the boy's raised hands, and gives it back to the girl, who is red and disheveled from crying. Then he takes Silvestrs firmly by the shoulders and shakes him.

"Didn't you hear what Mom said?" he asks sternly.

Silvestrs doesn't answer and just tries to break free from his father's grip. Dita feels sorry for him, after all he's just a child, but she doesn't meddle in men's affairs. She looks at her husband's tall, sinewy form, his slightly hunched back, his black hair graying at the temples, and tries to find something else inside of her that bonds them to each other. But there isn't anything. Just their loan, the house, and five—no, six—children. Looking at any of her daughters or sons, Dita always feels something big, something expansive and warm. She wants to watch over and protect them, to take care of and embrace them. But her husband . . . Sometimes watching Niks from the sidelines, it seems to Dita like mere coincidence that she's living under the same roof with this stranger, whom she's shared a bed with for eighteen years. He's never told her "I love you." Or if he has, Dita has forgotten about it.

Dita pours some water into a bowl and takes it into the empty room. Closing the door carefully behind her, she puts the dish down onto the sheets—in front of the cat's nose. Minna stops fidgeting, her bed flecked with rosy discharge, and greedily drinks the cool, clean water. Dita feels around cautiously—one. The kitten squeaks and its mother immediately stops drinking and pokes her nose over to see if her little one is safe.

"Don't worry, Minna dear, I won't hurt him," Dita whispers and strokes Minna's side. The spasms start again; the cat tenses up, and Dita lets Minna rub her nose anxiously against her palm. Minna purrs as she convulses, she seems to choke for a second, and then Dita sees another small, slimy lump slide out, lifting its head and trying to breathe. Without looking around, the mother cat begins quickly and carefully licking the tiny, calico body and nose until the little creature begins to squeak and, rocking its head, crawls deeper on shaky little legs into its mother's fur.

Dita puts the water bowl on the floor close to the cat's bed and walks out again, quietly shutting the door.

While the smoked pork ribs are bubbling away in the big pot, Dita puts ten eggs in the smaller kettle to boil, peels the potatoes, grates the carrots, and uses a sharp knife to chop the onions and the small, firm sorrel leaves that had grown in their own garden that spring. A mix of anger, guilt, and annoyance stews inside her as she thinks about the loan. They used that money to remodel part of the house—there wasn't enough for all of it. The children are well fed, clothed, the older ones each have a computer and a good phone. Marts is serious about hockey, which is an expensive sport, and her father had bought Asnate a real violin, so she doesn't have to screech away on a cheap one bought online. Asnate has a knack for it, she also participates in competitions abroad and her teachers have high hopes for her. Nobody could say that the money had been spent foolishly. If they'd kept it in the back of their minds and planned a bit, it's also not like they couldn't have made some regular payments on the loan. Niks is a good mechanic, he earns enough. But something else has always seemed more important, more urgent. Somewhere deep down inside she knows that she only has herself to blame. And Niks. Together with the accumulated interest, they're up to twenty-five thousand. They don't have money like that, even if they sold the house. This thought makes Dita shake.

"Hey Mom!"

Asnate's blonde head appears for a moment in the hallway and then disappears into the girls' room.

"Your brothers didn't come home with you?" Dita calls after the girl. No answer. She's probably plugged her ears up with her headphones again. But headphones are actually a good thing.

32

Dita didn't even want to imagine the din that would fill the house if everybody was loudly listening to whatever they liked best. But it's hard to have a conversation that way; everyone off in their own world, staring at a computer or phone.

Dita is grating some boiled eggs and looking out the window. It's stopped raining and just now she sees the boys; it's a surprise that the two of them are together. Roberts usually doesn't like being around his brother. Marts still seems too childish and chatty to him. Especially when he starts getting carried away, talking about his workouts and using his whole body to show different moves. But right now, as they're talking to each other, they seem friendly and relaxed. Dita feels her chest swell with warmth again.

A bird lands on the windowsill in the kitchen. A small, gray bird. So plain as to be easily missed. Dita knows nearly every bird. Living here at the edge of the forest she knows almost all its residents just by their faces. But this isn't a thrush, a finch, a flycatcher, or a nuthatch. So tiny—a sort Dita has never seen before. It stands, clutching the ridged tin with its delicate claws, and studies her with one eye, then the other. Dita tries to move closer; the bird flits its tail up and down, but doesn't fly away.

"Hey, who are you? Did you bring me any news?" Dita whispers to herself and smiles, and for a moment imagines that the little bird is just as small and vulnerable as her unborn child.

Everything is cooking on the gas stove. The meat is done—deboned and sliced into small strips, the sorrel is cut into pieces, and the eggs are grated. When the potatoes have finished cooking in the broth, everything will get poured into the pot and the soup will be done. The sound of a violin picks up from behind the wall. Asnate first plays a few exercises but then starts playing a particular composition. Dita isn't familiar with classical music, but as she's walked around hearing her daughter's concerts, she's begun to listen more closely and feel the music. A beautiful, graceful melody flows from the next room until it suddenly stops in the middle of a measure. Asnate starts again from the beginning but stops again at the same place. And does the same again one more time after that. Asnate's playing usually doesn't bother Dita, but this time she feels herself getting nauseous again. Dita checks to see if the potatoes are done and walks out into the yard. They'll need to cook for at least ten more minutes.

Niks is working on something in the tool shed. He can't stay still for a second. Marts is growing up to be the same. Dita moves closer and sees the two of them working together. The yard is soaked with rain, making it impossible to work outside. But there's no end to the work that needs to be done. It's springtime. Dita walks up to the open shed and watches her husband's and son's movements. They don't speak much but their actions are coordinated and rhythmic. Niks takes an unfinished board and, turning it gently, places it in the middle of the workspace without looking, and Marts is already there, taking hold of it, and moving it to the other end of the room. It isn't clear to Dita what's happening or why, but she watches their clockwork movements with a smile. Niks turns, but this time notices his smiling wife standing in the doorway and smiles back at her. Dita's nausea has passed, and she returns to the kitchen.

*

In the evening, Dita crawls into bed with Niks. He is still awake and pulls her closer to him with his warm arms. Dita gives in and settles into the bend formed by his wiry frame.

"Tomorrow, I'll go to the bank. We need to figure out what we can do, what they can offer," Niks says quietly.

"And what if they don't want to be reasonable?"

"Then we'll have to think about it some more. Maybe I can go work for a year in Denmark. They need construction workers there. I know how to do it. At least we could pay off part of the debt. But I bet we'll be able to make a deal. I'm sure we could scratch up a hundred or so a month."

Dita tries to do the math in her head and figure out how long they'll have to keep paying if they can afford to give the bank a hundred euros a month. But she doesn't know or really understand how interest works and all her calculations fall apart. Niks's hands and body are very warm. Dita presses closer to him and feels him respond.

"You know, Minna had three kittens today," she starts to say hoping that the subject of their conversation will turn to their own child on the way. But Niks is already caressing her breasts and this time he pulls her nightie all the way off. Dita gets quiet. Her nipples are very sensitive and hurt a little, but even so she feels that she wants this and that somewhere deep down her desire has awoken—and that this time she wants her husband inside of her. They make love slowly and gently. Dita's entire body—from head to toe—grows warm, her cheeks and knees are burning, and the very core of her body starts pulsing stronger and stronger until it explodes in rhythmic waves, clenching around Niks's member. And then he pushes deeper, a bit deeper still until with a stifled groan he enters the depths of his wife's body, emptying out inside of her, and then relaxes and remains lying on her body.

"Is that okay, does it hurt?" he asks.

Dita feels a slight tug in her lower abdomen, a mix of pain and pleasurable release, but she answers:

"No, it's fine."

Niks lies down next to her and pulls her closer, but is asleep at almost the same instant. Dita thinks for a moment about Niks possibly going abroad for work. But now she feels afraid, she doesn't want to be all alone with the children, the coming birth, the house, and everything in it. She presses closer to Niks and falls asleep.

The next morning Niks is already up when Dita awakes to a worrying feeling. The tugging pain hasn't stopped. Every ten minutes a small but subtly painful shiver runs down Dita's body and then stops again.

"I'll take the older kids to school," Niks opens the door and tells Dita. She looks at her husband and feels annoyed, they shouldn't have made love last night and now she's hurting because of it. But she had wanted it too. Dita's mind is a mess, and she feels a kind of fear in her heart that she can't quite define.

"Niks, maybe let them walk, I think I need to see the doctor. I'll drive with you, I just won't be able to get ready fast enough for everybody to go at the same time."

Niks eyes his wife intently and closes the door. Dita hears the kids groan unhappily, but then the door slams and the three oldest are gone. Dita gets out of bed naked and puts on her nightie to walk to the shower, but notices brown streaks on the sheets. Her heart starts beating faster, Dita wipes her groin with the corner of the white nightie. Thick, dark brown discharge stains the clean, white cotton cloth, and now Dita feels really scared.

"Niks!" she calls out and her husband opens the door right away. "Niks, I'm going to take a shower. Take the little ones over to your mom's."

Niks looks confused as he stares at Dita's dirty nightie and still doesn't understand what's happening. But he goes to Silvestrs and Dārta right away to get them dressed and take them over to his mother's. It's only three kilometers, he'll be back soon. Dita hears Niks calling his mother to warn her as he heads out the door.

Dita adjusts the water to a lukewarm temperature and gets into the shower. She feels her stomach contort, she bends over and waits for a moment.

"Please hold on, little one. I won't do that again, just hold on, okay? Please, hold on, please," she murmurs quietly and strokes her abdomen with light, gentle movements. After washing she looks down and everything is white and clean, it seems like there is no more discharge.

Dita gets out of the shower. Suddenly, something hot pours down her legs, splashes across the bathroom floor, and wrenches her over in pain. Leaning forward she sees her blood-stained legs and feels her child ripping its way through her until it breaks free and slides from her groin, sloshing like a mucousy hunk of meat onto the tile floor. The sharp pain passes. With an empty head and empty stomach, Dita watches the gently trembling lump, which had seconds ago been part of her. It is a little larger than the mother cat's newborn kitten, and the first thought that runs through her mind is "maybe it's still alive, maybe the doctor can somehow put it back, maybe they can save it somehow . . ."

No, she reluctantly comes back to reality. No. It's over.

Dita, still naked, finds paper towels in the cabinet—her hands shaking—and collects everything that can be collected. The door opens, Niks face appears, but catching sight of his blood-stained wife and the floor, he quickly shuts it again.

"Should I call the paramedics?" he asks through the closed door.

"No need, what's the use, we'll leave in a minute . . ." Dita answers in a trance and continues gathering together all the bits of mucous and flesh, everything that can be picked up and wrapped in napkins. A melody, just a few bars, keeps gently running through her head on constant repeat, and she hums along under her breath. She loves her child, her little bird, she loves him and is singing just for him. Dita puts everything she's collected off the floor into a shoebox she found on the windowsill, wipes the floor with a rag, her hands now extremely weak, and gets in the shower to rinse off again.

Before they go, Dita sticks the box into the central heating furnace and turns it on in a daze. Tightly shutting the tiny furnace door, she locks up the house and gets in the car. Niks puts his hand on her shoulder, and she shivers involuntarily. Then he puts both of his hands on the steering wheel and drives.

They merge onto the highway that goes to the city. Niks seems calm but every now and again he shoots a sideways glance toward Dita. After a week and a half of rain, the sun has finally broken through the clouds and is shining right in their eyes. Dita closes hers.

"Are you okay?" Niks asks. The sun paints his wife's face in golden hues and illuminates the delicate fuzz on her cheeks. Dita is still beautiful, but so frail.

"Okay? What could possibly be okay? Niks, we just lost our child! You understand, that baby is no more. Do you even get it? Do you care?" Dita doesn't have the strength to yell, but her eyes are now wide open as she stares at Niks.

"Listen. That wasn't a child, not yet! And, no, I don't care that we won't have it. I've got five more kids, and this was not a child!" Niks spits out each word. "And the only thing I care about is that you're okay, that you're not in pain, that you don't bleed to death, that you're alive and well. You're important to me, don't you get it?"

But Dita doesn't hear the last sentences. Niks doesn't care that their child is gone. Niks is unconcerned that their baby— their little bird—is dead. How could she have ever loved this kind of a man. He hasn't said he loves her even once, he is empty, even emptier than her womb. Dita doesn't say a word the rest of the way to the hospital. Niks's hands clench the steering wheel so tightly that his knuckles have turned completely white and his driving is distracted, but even so, he soon pulls into a parking space at the hospital.

"The cat is in the empty room. She had her kittens yesterday. Let her out to walk, but make sure she gets back in to see them."

"And put out some clean water for her. The kids don't know yet," Dita says, takes her purse, gets out, and walks away without looking back.

"Call me when you're ready to come home," Niks calls after her but can't tell whether Dita heard him or not.

They perform a dilation and curettage on Dita and the doctor recommends she spend the night at the hospital.

"You're not as young as you used to be, we need to watch you a bit," she says.

It seems to Dita that the doctor is a little perplexed and that her voice is laced with something like a hint of guilt. A week ago, everything was completely fine, all of the tests perfect, she couldn't have missed anything, right . . .

But Dita doesn't tell the doctor everything. She doesn't tell her that she thought about how Niks is apathetic, doesn't tell her that she'd dreamed about what it would be like to sleep with someone else but still ended up sleeping with her own husband. And how strong the convulsions had been in her uterus that night, stronger than any of the other times she'd conceived a child. There's no reason to tell her any of that, her child is gone. And Dita is responsible for all of it, she doesn't even know what she wants or what she doesn't.

Dita spends the night in the hospital ward, falling from time to time into a fitful sleep only to have the same dream over and over again. She's giving birth to a large, healthy child, the maternity ward's glass doors are closed, and Niks is standing behind them. She's giving birth and sees Niks's mouth opening and closing, he looks anxious and worried, but she can't hear what he's yelling. Every time she strains to hear what her husband is saying over the child's crying, she wakes up. She's alone in the hospital ward, light from streetlamps is streaming in through the window, and everything is quiet. Closer to the morning she falls into a dreamless sleep and wakes up only when the nurse brings her breakfast.

While lying awake at night, Dita thinks about the ashes in their furnace at home. She'll scatter them under the apple tree. So she knows where the child is . . . Dita can't even explain why she needs that. But she does. Hopefully Niks won't have burned anything else in the furnace in the meantime.

Dita doesn't want to call Niks, doesn't want to talk to him, and comes home the next day by bus. The younger kids must be at her mother-in-law's, the older ones at school. Niks isn't at home either, he's definitely working. Dita doesn't look into the furnace right away and goes to the empty room first. Minna is still curled up in the same box, but when Dita enters she lifts her head and lets out a friendly meow. Her water dish is full, and food has also been put down for her. Two tiny forms lie in the curve of the mother cat's body—both of them calico like Minna herself, but the third, completely white, is stretched out a short distance away. Dita strokes the white one with two fingers, the kitten is warm and soft. But it doesn't move. The mother cat gets out of her bed and walks over to Dita. The calico kittens press closer to each other as they sleep, but the white one stays stretched out. Dita watches cautiously and doesn't touch him again.

She gets a clay bowl and the small ash shovel and walks over to the furnace. She opens the door and stares for a moment.

It's not clear if anything else had been burned, the side of the furnace is cool, but it cools quickly. Dita decides not to ask her husband about it. She scoops the ashes from the furnace and pours them into the bowl, one shovelful, a second, a third.

"Hi, little one," she addresses the ashes softly. "Hi," she says again and doesn't know what more to say.

If she hadn't thought the wrong thoughts, if she hadn't given into her desire, her child would still be alive inside her. Her feelings of guilt are grinding down and crushing her, Dita's hands are tired, but she takes the bowl and carries it out to the yard. Minna follows her everywhere, not even dropping back for an instant. They walk together out to the young apple tree behind the house. Stopping along the way, Dita picks some wild tulips that are growing on the south side and lays them across the bowl. She puts the rather heavy vessel on the ground and sits down underneath the apple tree. And then she gently scatters the ashes a handful at a time onto the grass. There's not a single thought in her head, only silence, until it is gradually interrupted by a delicate, resonant whistling. Dita looks up—yesterday's little gray bird is perched singing on a branch of the apple tree. It then falls silent, shakes its stubby tail, jumps from branch to branch at lightning speed, and whistles again—sonorously and without a care. Dita finishes scattering the ashes, gets up, lays the tulips over them, and stands for a moment with her eyes closed, her face turned toward the sun. The little bird whistles and whistles, and when Dita opens her eyes, the gentle breeze has scattered the ashes, covering the grass and yellow flowers like a white frost.

A car rumbles into the yard. The little gray bird takes flight, flaps its wings to hover in place for a moment, then flies up straight into the air, disappearing behind the old apple trees. Dita takes the ash-dusted bowl and heads to the yard. Niks catches sight of his wife and looks at her with large exhausted eyes. He wants to say something, but a happy Dārta practically tumbles out of the car and calls out:

"Mom, where were you? We've got kittens in the empty room!"

Dita puts the bowl under the bench by the house, Silvestrs also immediately scrambles out of the car, and both of the little ones each take Dita by the hand and lead her toward the house to show her the kittens. Dita's palms and clothing are dusty, and she doesn't want to speak with Niks right away, so she gives in and goes into the empty room with the children. Their little hands are smudged with ashes. Minna sneaks in with them and climbs back into her bed. Both of the calico kittens lift their trembling little heads and crawl squeaking into their mother's fur looking for a teat. Only the white one is still where it was. Dita's legs go weak, she understands that the white one is dead; he hasn't moved in at least half an hour. Dita wants to push the kids out of the room, so they don't see, and she is afraid to touch the kitten. He is already cool.

But Dārta runs up and pokes the white one with a finger. The kitten extends its tiny paws in all directions and, after a good stretch, yawns and rolls over from one side to the other. Dārta grabs the little kitten with her ash-stained hand and sticks it nose-first into the fur of Minna's belly.

Dita can't take it anymore, her vision clouds over, she feels everything burst open—she feels it in her eyes, her breasts, her head—everything that had been building up since yesterday, but in reality for much longer, it gushes out like a torrent, all of it at once and in every direction—running down her cheeks, pouring out onto her hands—consecrated by ash—which are raised to cover her mouth, dripping onto Dārta's fair hair and into the mother cat's fur. Through her tears Dita sees Silvestrs looking frightened as he watches her, and then feels him lean into her. But at the same moment Dita also feels safe, strong hands grip her shoulders. And then she suddenly remembers what Niks had said in the car yesterday. "You're important to me." She can't speak but presses close, so close to her husband and hides her face in his rough sweater, impenetrable to her tears.

"Why didn't you call?" Niks asks. He's quiet for a moment as he hugs his crying wife, then adds: "I arranged everything with the bank yesterday. One hundred sixty euros a month. We'll make it through."

ALEKSANDRA IS BEAUTIFUL

Aleksandra rolls her chair slowly and carefully down the hill. Her arms are used to it and trained for it, and the return trip uphill doesn't frighten her. If there's anything that's giving her caution, it's the clouds building on the horizon. But she nevertheless continues on her way. A few more weeks and winter will be here. Then she'll be trapped inside those four walls for longer—traveling on icy paths in a wheelchair is pretty nightmarish. And the mountains of snow piled up along the street and the edge of the sidewalk are nearly impassable. She has to keep moving, has to take advantage of every chance to get outside. Aleksandra shoots another glance at the darkening heavens and shivers imagining a trip through the rain, turning the wet, muddy wheels. Gloves protect the skin of her strong hands from blisters and bruises, but in wet weather, mud splatters in every direction and there's no way to protect against that. But that's nothing compared to her first trips out in spring when the melting snow transforms into a slurry of mud and feces. Aleksandra doesn't have a sufficiently polite word in her vocabulary to refer to the sidewalks and paths covered in all the dog waste that had been preserved in snow over the course of the winter, only to sink to ground level during the thaw. When you want to go outside so badly, lift your face toward the sun, flare your nostrils, breathe in the first aromas of spring and finally get a chance to really move around, and you—you're only human after all—can't wait any more and go for a ride just as the snow starts to melt, and just wind up twisting and straining your hands, your head down, maneuvering between piles of shit, trying to keep the wheels clean since you have to turn them with your hands and afterward you have to be able to take the chair inside again . . . God damn all those mongrels, mutts, and cats too! People don't have enough problems already without surrounding themselves with these totally pointless creatures. Well, she could understand if someone needed to protect their property or used a dog to track a criminal or someone who had gone missing, but, come on, just keeping weird, yapping fleabags and yowling furballs at home for no reason. What's the point? And then all that running around to the vet and pet store. When she was a child, her grandmother out in the countryside would give the dog the same food as people, leftovers from their own table. And the dog was sweet, but still knew its place and responsibilities as a dog. What changed?

Aleksandra lets out a wicked laugh about herself. Such an idiot. It hasn't even snowed once yet and here she is ruining her mood, fuming about the spring shit. And her grumbling has already come down to cat and dog owners . . .

Aleksandra is beautiful. A tall, athletic body in a white knit sweater, a white hat, a colorful scarf that she had knitted herself, and thick, dark hair flowing lavishly down her shoulders. Her riding gloves also match her outfit—white with an embroidered pattern, the orange protective leatherette layer covering the palms the same color as the tangerine stripe in her scarf. And that's how it always is—everything is carefully considered and coordinated down to the finest detail.

Pretty, but still grumbling, Aleksandra rolls on. The road drives her forward. She has today all planned out.

*

It's almost three. Two more hours and Dagnija will be able to mount her "steed"—that's what she calls her bike—and shoot across town toward home. Her car usually sits unused during the summer and fall months when she can walk around town, and if she's got her steed then it feels like practically a sin to ferry herself around on some soft cushioned seat. Maybe she should stop at Aleksandra's? She hasn't been answering her phone all morning. Dagnija doesn't want to be a bother. She calls twice a day, sometimes more, but only if there's an actual reason. But when Aleksandra doesn't pick up or call her back, she starts to get nervous and carries her phone around everywhere in her pocket. She typically doesn't do that and is usually much more forgetful with it. Plus, who would even be calling her? Aside from her contact with Aleksandra, her phone sometimes sits silent for weeks.

Dagnija had noticed Aleksandra around town some time ago, though she knew nothing about her. Always alone, always so well put together and elegant. She was so beautiful that every time Dagnija encountered her, she gazed at the stranger in the

47

wheelchair with both admiration and humility as if she were an untouchable and unattainable work of art that could only be admired from afar.

And then the day came. Dagnija works as a librarian, and it was her turn to run to the bakery nearby to pick up some pastries for the coffee break. Leaving the library, she suddenly stumbled on the perfectly level ground. There, sitting in her wheelchair in the cobblestone square by the colorful dahlia patch, was her object of interest, staring intently at the three steep steps leading up to the library's main entrance.

"Hello, can I help you?" Dagnija was out of breath and her heart was racing, but she still gathered up the courage to address the stranger.

"That would be nice," Aleksandra answered calmly and coolly. "You could ask one of the employees to come outside, since it looks like I probably won't be able to get in."

Dagnija felt guilty that the library had no elevator, no lifting device, not even just a ramp. The building was an unrenovated, generic, Soviet-era office building. Twenty-five years ago, the library moved here from a small wooden building on the edge of town and back then the walls were just given a fresh coat of paint and new linoleum put down in its rooms. She remembered that even that seemed a bit too fancy back then . . .

"I'm a librarian," Dagnija finally managed to blurt out while blushing slightly.

"Fantastic, then maybe you'll know if you have a book on mitten designs? It's new, just recently published. It was gone from the bookstores within two months, I didn't manage to get there in time."

Yes, Dagnija knew they had that book in their collection, but it was checked out right now. How nice, Dagnija already felt her chest tighten and tremble with joy as she imagined taking the book straight to this patron's house, knowing how delighted she'd surely be.

"You're not a library member yet? Then you should sign up, I can do it right here, I'll just run in to get a form and card. Can you wait? If not, you can leave your address and I can stop by tonight after work," Dagnija—speaking effusively—realized that she was probably going a bit too far or, more precisely, too intimate, and quickly continued: "But we can also do that when the book gets here, then I can come to you with the book and the registration form."

Aleksandra listened to Dagnija's torrent of words, tilting her head slightly, and, it seemed to Dagnija, smirking with disinterest. The thick curls of her black hair above her forehead cast a shadow over her eyes.

"Thank you. As you can see, I can get here myself. There's no need to come to my house." Her voice seemed to have a mocking tone, or maybe it only seemed that way to Dagnija. "I'll leave my number, call me when the book is available."

Reaching behind to the backpack hanging from the back of her wheelchair, she pulled a bright green pen and notepad from its top pocket, wrote something down, and carefully tore out the page with the writing.

"Mitten Patterns. Aleksandra. 5178 3307," Dagnija read the information written firmly in block letters across the graph paper page. Aleksandra, what a name! Just as noble and aristocratic as its bearer. At that moment, Dagnija didn't yet know that Aleksandra only allows herself to be called by her full name—never Sandra, Sasha, or Sana, though Dagnija never would have thought to carve any nickname from this name worthy of a goddess.

"I'll call you as soon as the book is here," she declares, hiding her disappointment about the rejection.

And the most beautiful person that Dagnija had ever met turned around to roll away. Dagnija froze, desperately searching her mind for some scenario or possibility to stop her, to arrange another meeting, to overcome herself, schedule a visit, maybe help with something, to . . .

Aleksandra looked so strong and independent that Dagnija didn't dare utter a word. To offer her help might seem like she was trying to diminish her, to show her own superiority, but that's not what Dagnija wanted. Not at all.

All she could do was wait until the mitten patterns gave her the chance to be close to Aleksandra at least one more time, to talk to her, to be needed by her even if only for a moment. Dagnija had never wanted to be near another person this much. She couldn't understand it.

That was at the end of last summer. And then a miracle happened. No, it was actually Dagnija slowly, cautiously, and carefully creating her own miracle . . . When Aleksandra came to get the book, Dagnija had already spoken with the head of the library about access, and while she was standing in the courtyard next to the dahlia bed, she was able to tell Aleksandra that a petition had been submitted and that the city council was in support of constructing a ramp and automatic door, they just had to wait until next year's budget. Aleksandra listened and smiled. Dagnija couldn't interpret Aleksandra's smile, sometimes it seemed to glint with a hint of mockery, though maybe that was just a defense mechanism developed unconsciously over the years; Dagnija knew all the challenges that Aleksandra had to deal with every single day . . .

Dagnija had been married once. Mārtiņš had been good— such a big, warm, and cozy person. They had grown up in apartments next door from each other, played together, gone to school together—though Mārtiņš was two years ahead of her. When the other girls in her seventh-grade class started to talk about boys, the color surging and draining from their faces when they were near them, going on dates, making new friends, feuding and squabbling out of jealousy or passion, Dagnija could only watch and marvel. She had Mārtiņš, who was with her through thick and thin even before she ever began thinking about marriage. But Dagnija didn't feel weak in the knees, get butterflies in her stomach, or anything else that the other girls whispered about to each other.

"You've got Mārtiņš, that's why you don't care about anything else," they'd say.

Yes, she had Mārtiņš, and Mārtiņš had her, and they both knew that it was "till death do us part." No passion, no jealousy—so, Dagnija remained ignorant of them. Mārtiņš was like a brother, like a best friend, she could curl up next to him when she was tired or sad—or for no particular reason at all. To get warm. It was hard to believe when, two years after their wedding, he started to complain about persistent fatigue, about seeing black spots. Some time passed before Dagnija convinced him to go to the doctor, and they were shocked when the diagnosis came a few months later—multiple sclerosis. Everything happened so fast.

"The disease tends to be especially aggressive in men, but we'll do whatever we can," the neurologist said to Dagnija without looking her in the eyes when she had arrived at the hospital to take her husband home again.

She was ready to sacrifice whatever it took, but Mārtiņš quickly lost his strength, his legs stopped listening to him, he was hospitalized eight times over the course of the year. Nothing helped, the disease did not let up for even an instant, and her big, strong husband wasted away before her eyes. He wouldn't eat, was angry at the doctors, at life, at Dagnija, who tore herself apart trying to take care of wheelchair-bound Mārtiņš and to keep up a sense of optimism and faith in his recovery . . . A week before their fifth wedding anniversary, Mārtiņš caught pneumonia and, despite his doctors' desperate fight, died two days later.

Mārtiņš was buried on their wedding anniversary. Dagnija knew already then that she would never remarry. Her mom said:

"It's good that you didn't have a child, it'll be easier alone, you'll find somebody."

Dagnija was angry, used to caring, helping, fussing over someone, and now she was left hanging—nobody needed her. At least if she'd had a child . . . But she neither needed, nor wanted "somebody."

She had been living a quiet, lonely, and monotonous life for sixteen years now.

"I could help Aleksandra with so much, with everything I know about the day-to-day lives of people in wheelchairs and how to take care of them," Dagnija thought sadly.

If they met on the street, Aleksandra would usually smile and wave, but they wouldn't talk. Or to be more precise, Dagnija never initiated a conversation, but gradually memorized the times and places where "accidental encounters" were the most likely. Another time, already late into the fall, Aleksandra needed a different knitting book; she called, the book was on the shelf, and Dagnija once again met her perfect woman by the now-empty flower bed, this time dressed in a warm windbreaker and mittens.

And then suddenly the snow arrived. It was a strange winter, atypical for Latvia, the snow fell in mid-November and didn't melt completely until the end of March.

"A wonderful winter, such a wonderful winter," thought Dagnija as she rang Aleksandra for their now-regular once-weekly call to ask if she needed anything, and usually receiving detailed instructions to bring something from the store, the pharmacy, or sometimes the self-service parcel machine. Aleksandra had a helper from social services who came twice a week to mop the floor, brush out the corners of the ceiling with a long broom, and also to go the store in winter, but it seemed that Aleksandra didn't fully trust her, and had never asked her to bring a croissant or lemon éclair from the bakery, or the expensive blue cheese from the fancy product shelves at the supermarket. And certainly, she had never invited her to enjoy any of those goodies with her over a cup of wonderfully aromatic black tea. She would invite Dagnija now and again and serve them out of her fancy gold-rimmed tea service decorated with red poppies. Those were very happy days.

Aleksandra talked about her life. She'd been in the chair for twenty-four years, next summer she'll be able to celebrate her silver anniversary, she laughed. A drunk driver had hit her with his truck two days after her university graduation. After receiving her posting, she would have been a specialist at the statistics board in Riga, as she had some of the highest marks in her graduating class.

"I was pretty, smart, and flirted like the devil himself, the boys swarmed around me like bees to honey. But I didn't have anyone special, I thought there would be time for all that . . . After the accident, all the bees were gone, scattering every which way—like cockroaches in the light."

They both laughed about the fitting comparison, but Dagnija watched the well-defined smile lines in the corners of Aleksandra's mouth and her just barely noticeable double chin, soft like a mouse's stomach, under her sculpted jawline, and thought quietly how Aleksandra was still beautiful, the most beautiful woman she had ever met.

"It's good that I had my mom during the first years, that she was with me while I learned that I could live this way and that I have to live life how it actually is. In the beginning I thought I'd walk again . . . I'd spend every day stewing in anger and hatred, but then in disappointment."

"Do you hate that driver?"

"It depends on the day. Sometimes. More often I'm sorry for him. He served his sentence in jail, and during that time he lost his family—his wife left him for someone else and then took the kids and moved away from Latvia. And so he kept drinking. He ruined his own life."

"And yours . . ." Dagnija thought to herself.

Entering Aleksandra's apartment for the first time, Dagnija was surprised how meticulous its layout was. Over the last year she'd gotten used to it, but she still admired Aleksandra for all she had planned out and done so she could live there with as little help from others as possible. Much of the space in the two-room apartment was open. Some furniture stood along the walls but reached no higher than midway up the wall with only a few paintings higher up than that. The doorways had been widened, the doors removed. The setup for getting in and out, getting up and moving around the bedroom and bathroom were all designed by Aleksandra, who had improved on the generic equipment available to the wheelchair-bound. During the course of the remodel, she had ruthlessly fired several handymen until the end result fully satisfied their moody customer. But only someone who couldn't or didn't want to understand Aleksandra's day-to-day life would ever think to call her moody.

When Mārtiņš was in his wheelchair, there really wasn't time to think about how to transform their apartment so that his daily life, which had been deformed by illness, would be made easier and more comfortable. Things happened too quickly and Dagnija tried to do everything for Mārtiņš that he couldn't do anymore for himself. That's why she truly understood and appreciated the importance of every tiny nuance in the arrangement of Aleksandra's place and was fully convinced of her genius.

Dagnija stops and gets off her bike as she approaches Aleksandra's house. Her heart is racing as she fumbles through her purse for her cell phone. She slowly pieces together the number from memory, but her finger hesitates over the green button. If anybody asked, Dagnija wouldn't be able to explain her feelings rationally. But she pulls herself together, quickly pushes the call button and lifts the phone up to her ear. She hears it ringing and as usual Dagnija counts the rings—one, two, three . . . eight . . . eleven, twelve. Disappointed she hangs up, climbs back onto her steed again, and keeps riding. But after passing a few more streets she can't wait anymore and without hesitating this time tries calling again. She lets it ring longer than before. No answer. That's never happened. Aleksandra always has her cell phone within arm's reach—her health is not stable enough to take any risks. And she's a light sleeper. Dagnija would definitely be less concerned if she heard a sullen, sleepy voice on the other end, instead of these indifferent, irritating beeps. Dagnija is confused. Unsure of the best course of action, she stands on the street and hesitates, but finally decides to go home, where she pushes her bike into the apartment entrance hall and makes herself some hawthorn tea to calm her nerves. But her worry doesn't go away. Aleksandra's apartment keys are in the kitchen-table drawer. At some point she'd given them to Dagnija and had said with a smirk:

"If I really did die, the corpse brigade will have to get in here somehow."

Picking up the phone, Dagnija hesitates again. It could be anything . . . Very rarely—maybe three times during the last year—Aleksandra has had a guest and didn't want to be disturbed, but then she would just shut off her phone. Dagnija knows nothing about this mystery guest and when she asks, Aleksandra just says, "You don't need to know," and then doesn't say another word. After the guest leaves, Aleksandra is a bit more testy than usual for a few days, and more distracted. Also more melancholy. But her guest never stays for more than a few hours and never spends the night. That's why Dagnija calls again. And again after fifteen minutes. And again.

By eight Dagnija is in a panic. Nobody is picking up at Aleksandra's number, and her anxiety has taken over her whole mind, not leaving a single corner free for other thoughts. Taking the spare keys and saying the Lord's Prayer, Dagnija gets into her little silver Opal and drives carefully out onto the road.

She parks her car in the courtyard of Aleksandra's building and carefully studies the windows and loggia. The apartment is on the first floor. Completely dark. She sticks her hand into her pocket and closes it tightly over the keys. She has to go. Maybe Aleksandra needs help. Yes, she has to go.

Ringing the doorbell a few times, Dagnija anxiously fidgets with the keys in her hand. There's no other option. The key slides easily into the lock; Aleksandra always locks it so it's possible to get in from the outside. For the same safety reasons—and if she manages to make a call but can't make it to the door. After turning the key halfway, the pin tumblers stick. For a moment, Dagnija thinks that something might have broken, but then she turns the handle. The door wasn't locked . . .

The apartment is dark and stinks.

"Aleksandra!"

She steps in warily.

"Aleksandra! It's Dagnija. Are you home?" She fumbles her way through the entrance hall to the bedroom.

She feels around until she finds the light switch next to the door and, turning it on, immediately sees the disorderly bed, but Aleksandra isn't in it. Her wheelchair is sitting askew on the other side . . . Dagnija slowly moves forward. She has crossed a boundary by coming in uninvited, her sense of discomfort creeping up her neck like a hairy caterpillar and she can't shake it.

Then she sees her. Aleksandra is lying on the floor between the wheelchair and bed, her cell phone—as expected—right there within arm's reach. Dagnija leans down, then gets on her knees, puts her palm on Aleksandra's her forehead, then checks her pulse—she is alive, warm, heart beating. And then Dagnija slowly realizes that the stink is emanating directly from Aleksandra. Aleksandra gently smacks her lips as she sleeps, saliva trickling down from the corner of her mouth and soaking into her hair—usually so well-groomed, but now sticky. Her soft, elegant, knit pants have slid halfway off her bottom; the powerful stench of urine hits Dagnija, mixing with a foul, suffocating funk. A little worried that she is doing something inappropriate, Dagnija uses both of her hands to take Aleksandra by the shoulders and shake her. She doesn't wake up, just keeps burping with eyes closed, and then it finally dawns on

Dagnija—Aleksandra is blackout drunk. Letting her go for a moment, Dagnija looks down perplexed at the helpless, reeking body on the floor. Aleksandra sighs, hiccups, and turns her torso to the side and resumes snoring.

Dagnija stands up and walks to the kitchen. The table is piled high with dishes and boxes of randomly scattered leftovers from various snacks. There's also an empty bottle of cognac. A plastic two-liter bottle with the remnants of some unidentifiable liquid. Dagnija unscrews and sniffs it. Moonshine. Two dirty glasses on the table, the floor is covered in dirty footprints—so somebody else had been here.

Dagnija sits down on a stool—confused and in disbelief at what she's seeing—and then tries to understand what to do next. She has to do something. But what?

Dagnija takes off her coat and returns to the bedroom. She stares at the sleeping Aleksandra for a moment and mutters:

"Drunk. Blackout drunk."

She can't leave Aleksandra in this state, she needs to roll up her sleeves, get her limp body into bed, and clean her up as much possible. She probably can't drag her to the bathroom— she judges the distance and her own strength. No, she needs to do it some other way. Dagnija takes the blanket and pillows off the bed, grabs Aleksandra under the arms, and tries to get her up onto the mattress. It's unbelievable how heavy she actually is! Dagnija doesn't give up and grabs her more resolutely. She tries to maneuver her by supporting Aleksandra's butt against the side of the bed, pressing Aleksandra's upper body against her shoulder, and lifts with her knees to try and force Aleksandra's uncooperative form into bed. Dagnija hears something slosh and then feels it splash onto her hair, neck, shoulders, and back. Aleksandra has thrown up. A sour slurry drips over Dagnija and onto the floor. Dagnija pushes the unsteady mass of flesh into bed and runs to the bathroom, tearing off her coat—thank goodness it's zippered—as well as her bra, and, leaning over the edge of the bathtub, rinses off and washes her hair under the tap. She stuffs her filthy clothing into a plastic bag she'd found in the bathroom, lightly rinsing it off first, and then returns to the bedroom, naked from the waist up. Aleksandra is asleep, snoring, and in the same position in which Dagnija had left her.

Dagnija goes and locks the door. She leaves the key in the lock so the it can't be unlocked from the outside. She strips completely naked. And then she gets to work.

Aleksandra is still asleep, sighing heavily and snorting from time to time. Dagnija has washed the floor in the kitchen and bathroom, washed the dishes, thrown the empty bottles and half-eaten snacks—sausage slices soaking in olive juice; broken, crumbling bits of bread; cubes of cheese sticky with finger-prints—into a garbage bag. She has wiped down every wet, sticky surface. Dagnija had never imagined that working na-ked could be so thrilling. Just regular everyday cleaning—the sponge lightly, accidentally touching the skin of her stomach; her nipple brushing the surface of the table as she bends over to wipe down its entire length; cold drops of water splashing onto her warm skin as water runs from the faucet into the sink, resulting in tiny little pearls of gooseflesh. A funny feeling, but Dagnija likes it . . .

When the rooms are clean again, Dagnija tries shaking Aleksandra awake one more time, but she's dead to the world. It's clear that she probably won't regain consciousness tonight. So, Dagnija has to pull off those stinking clothes and wash them herself, to whatever extent that's even possible. She knows how to do that, and it isn't too difficult if every movement is approached with kindness and care. She's become profoundly attached to Aleksandra, she's only had one other person as important in her life—her husband. But this time it feels different—more passionate, more vulnerable. At times, Dagnija has a hard time explaining why she feels as if she were walking on a knife's edge.

Dagnija brings water into the room—a big bowl, a small bowl, a bucket. She puts a towel underneath Aleksandra's head, rinses her dirty shocks of hair, dries them with a towel, washes her slobber-covered face with her hands, stroking her forehead and cheeks and gently drawing her finger across her lips. Then she undresses Aleksandra until she is also completely naked and, using a washcloth she'd found in the bathroom, cleans her entire body, every square centimeter, not even the tiniest spot on Aleksandra's body has gone untouched by Dagnija's hands . . . Every so often, Aleksandra's legs convulse in strange, spastic cramps, but she still doesn't wake.

After washing the floor around the bed, Dagnija pours out the dirty water and then sits down cross-legged on the wide bed next to her goddess. They are both naked, their proximity is electrifying, and Dagnija is shaking slightly from the excitement. This is the second time that she's seen Aleksandra without any clothes, so painfully beautiful and real with all her accident and surgery scars. It was in the summer when she called and offered Dagnija an adventure. For both of them to take the little Opal and drive out to the blooming poppy field to photograph themselves. It was so hot, after the first ten shots Aleksandra took off her blouse, afterward sitting there in only her bra, which was just as brilliantly red as the poppies . . . And then, laughing, she took that off too. Dagnija was confused, but watching this beautiful body through her camera's viewfinder was a lot easier than being this near, close enough to touch. Dagnija's photographs had turned out well, gentle yet alluring, even with all the scars . . .

It was already half past eleven. "I'm not going home," Dagnija decides as she sits next to Aleksandra. She isn't sure that she can leave Aleksandra alone. What if she throws up again and, heaven forbid, suffocates . . . There's plenty of room in the bed for two.

Dagnija lightly touches Aleksandra's now-dry black hair. It's stiffer and rougher than it looks, she hadn't noticed that when she was washing it. She brushes the soft tip of Aleksandra's nipple with her fingers. Shivers run from her hand all the way to her abdomen. Dagnija strokes Aleksandra's flat tummy. Then she takes her hand and puts it on her own breast, stomach, and below . . . She breathes deeply. Finally, she gets up, takes the blanket, turns out the light, and lies down next to Aleksandra; she doesn't touch her but slides her hand under her fragrant spread of hair . . . streetlight streams in through the window, making Aleksandra's profile appear dark yet wrapped in a fine, glittering halo. It seems like Dagnija will be able to fall asleep tonight.

*

Aleksandra reaches for the bowl next to the bed again and throws up the water she'd drunk. No, she doesn't blame herself. It's good that she drank at home, that she hadn't gone anywhere, that she hadn't fallen over somewhere in her chair, gotten hurt, felt ashamed. There had been times like that too, but thank God, those were long, long ago . . . Yeah, sometimes she'll drink a bit. Less and less often, now it might just be once every few years or even less often than that, but it happens. She still doesn't know any other way to shake herself up, knock herself out of her routine when her anger starts dominating everything else.

Moving slowly and with difficulty from the bed to the wheelchair and then rolling into the kitchen, she pours herself another glass of lemon water. It's good that last night's drunkenness hadn't stuck with her, getting over it can be even worse. She's sure in that case she wouldn't be able to resist a generous glug or two today, knowing that it would deliver her from a horrible hangover. Right after the accident, when she was learning how to live in a wheelchair, she drank practically every day, so she knows from experience how the hair of the dog can patch things up and make life bright again. Until the moment it gets to be too much. Thank God, for that, because looking for someone to bring you a bottle feels even more humiliating than puking up green vomit all day long . . .

When she woke that morning, she could feel a warm spot next to her. Someone had just left, Aleksandra probably woke from the sound of the door closing. The door was unlocked when she checked, but the apartment and her bed were clean, and she was had been washed and was even wearing a new pair of diapers. It clearly hadn't been the drinking buddy she'd met on the street last night. He probably wouldn't have wanted to sleep next to her, he probably couldn't even have . . . Though Aleksandra did see him craning his neck and staring from the kitchen when she was changing out of her outdoor clothes into the soft, comfortable track suit she wore at home. Last night when she'd passed out, he'd probably slunk off looking for more. Drinking away his sorrows, filthy, practically a bum. But when she'd met him on the street, the cognac was already in Aleksandra's shopping bag, getting drunk was already on the agenda, and she didn't care if she drank by herself or with company. And he'd flashed such a flirty, toothless grin at her that Aleksandra had to laugh.

"Well, what do you say, come over, let's knock one back!"

Once upon a time, he'd been a good-looking guy, an athlete, a good dancer. In his youth he could dance the waltz so elegantly that everyone else would flee the dance floor and watch with bated breath. But now he just babbled on aimlessly, repeating the same thing ten times over. It annoyed Aleksandra so much that she'd done shot after shot hoping to pass out sooner.

But it was clear that somebody else had been there overnight. Aleksandra couldn't remember how she'd gotten to her bedroom. If she really thought about it, she could probably figure out who had helped her, but if that person left without a trace, then what does it matter. She feels sick and isn't about to start playing detective. What's the point?

Her nausea retreats in the afternoon, her strength gradually returns, and Aleksandra opens the doors of the loggia. The late afternoon sun shines right in her face, and in helpless delight she closes her eyes and allows its rosy glow to dance across her skin and hair. The fresh air outside seems to flow in not only through her nose but also into every pore on her skin.

Suddenly something lands in her lap. Startled, Aleksandra opens her eyes. A cat! A black, adolescent cat, thin, bony, with long legs, large emerald eyes, and giant ears sticking straight up.

Unpleasantly startled, she exclaims "Where did you come from?" and jerks her hands away so as not to touch the creature. "What are you doing here? Are you lost, little one?"

But the cat just makes itself comfortable and starts purring. It stops, but then starts purring again and begins washing its coat. Well, that's just too much . . . Aleksandra is utterly confused, she's sitting with her hands up and doesn't know what to do. She can't stand cats, hates them. But this one is so affectionate and odd. He likes Aleksandra, would he have otherwise climbed into her lap? After cleaning himself up a bit, the little creature, still purring, curls up right there on her knees, blinking its eyes at her affectionately and licking itself a few more times, before slowly falling asleep. She watches the small, sniffling being and to her surprise feels a strange sort of tenderness awakening inside of her. She wants to protect it, love it. The cat is small, alone, and struggling with its circumstances, just like her. Aleksandra lowers her hands and slides her palm across the small, black ball of fur. Warm and sweet.

"Well, that's a surprise," she says quietly, more surprised by her own feelings than by the little cat that had appeared from who knows where.

"Well, let him sleep, but then he'll need to go back to wherever he came from," she whispers to herself and smiles.

She sits for nearly an hour guarding her little guest's slumber, watching the street outside her window, until the sun has nearly set. Cool air flows in through the open door, though there is no wind. Aleksandra stretches to get her warm shawl off the bed and puts it around her shoulders. That works, it'll do. Having slept its fill, the cat opens its eyes with a yawn, stretches, jumps off her lap, and walks out the loggia door without looking back. He leaps up onto the railing and disappears behind it. Aleksandra has an odd feeling as she closes the doors—a kind of dull ache, a kind of fear. Not for herself. But for the cat, which dove into the darkness, into the cold. So small and alone.

Aleksandra can't believe her eyes when she opens the loggia doors the next day: the little cat is there again and strides in self-confidently, its tail raised high. Just to nap there for an hour or two. The next day she is no longer surprised, but instead rolls over to the doors knowing that the cat will be waiting. He's there, of course, and starts visiting for longer spans, sniffing around and exploring every corner of her apartment, bolder and more shameless with each passing day, knocking down a flowerpot, on a different day taking the ball of yarn she was using to knit socks and completely unrolling it across the living room floor. Aleksandra fumes and laughs, wheeling after her little friend, chasing him around the apartment, threatening him with a kitchen towel, and waiting for the moment when the little guy will curl up in her lap, not doubting for a second that he could place his complete trust in this wheeled being.

On the fifth day, she rolls down to the supermarket and stops at the cat food display. Well, so be it, she decides. She also selects some elegant food dishes that match her apartment's décor, and a little cat bed. Ferdinands has found himself a home. Soon he also starts to spend nights in her apartment, and he gradually puts on weight until he becomes a rather stately little tomcat. Now and again Aleksandra has a good laugh at herself, remembering how stupid and strange people with cats at home had once seemed to her. Now she has a cat. Someone to smile at in the mornings, even though it was completely pointless. Cats don't understand smiles, it probably just looks to him like Aleksandra is baring her teeth. But even so she smiles at Ferdinands every morning, thinks how silly it is of her to do it, and then has a good laugh.

*

Christmas is coming. At no time has Dagnija hinted to Aleksandra that it was her who slept next to her that night. She doesn't know if Aleksandra noticed, saw, or sensed it back then. She should have noticed the next morning that someone had taken care of her, but does she know who? Only from time to time, when she glances over at Aleksandra, does Dagnija remember the feel of her palm against Aleksandra's smooth, warm skin. Her finger on Aleksandra's nipple. And smells the scent of her damp hair. The gentle tickle of her breath on her cheek in the dark of night. The feel of her bare breasts under her coat when she had left early that morning . . . A bundle of dirty clothes in her hands.

It has been snowing for a week, and this was to Dagnija's advantage. Aleksandra calls more often than at other times of the year for a favor or help—to go somewhere, to buy something, to take her somewhere in Dagnija's little Opal.

Right after that night, a cat showed up at Aleksandra's. Dagnija isn't any great animal lover, but still finds a way to establish a cordial relationship with anything that has a tail. But not this time. Ferdinands hates Dagnija. When she arrives, the cat sits down near her and carefully watches everything she does. Any time she makes a quick movement or gestures emphatically, the creature hisses and tries to swipe her with its paw. If it were Dagnija's cat, she would grab it by the scruff, throw it out, and close the door. But there aren't any doors on the rooms here, and Aleksandra's attitude is just generally pathological and would even seem funny if it didn't affect Dagnija. She never takes any interest in how Dagnija is doing, sure, she didn't do that before either, but then it just felt like nothing else mattered to her except her own body and life. But now Aleksandra can carry on for hours talking about how Ferdinands slept, how he played, how he understands her every word. The cat has been bought a fancy collar with a small, glittering crystal pendant. In contrast to the cool smiles that Aleksandra deigns to bestow on Dagnija, the cat is nuzzled, petted, cuddled. She whispers all kinds of sweet nothings into its ears, kisses its wet nose, and lets it lick her cheek, snuggle up to her breasts, and curl up on her lap. Dagnija would never have thought that there was this much affection and tenderness concealed within this pristine, cold beauty. And all of it goes to the cat . . . Anger boils over into rage in Dagnija's heart, and the animal probably senses that. When in her presence, Ferdinands curls up and falls asleep in the lap that belongs to him, it seems to Dagnija like the cat is coolly mocking her as it stares at her, its emerald eyes narrowed into slits . . .

It's snowing tonight again. Not large, heavy flakes, but it's still coming down without stopping. There's a light breeze. Along the way, her car window freezes shut, and the tires slide in a few spots, but Dagnija is a confident driver.

Aleksandra asked her to come that afternoon, but Dagnija couldn't get away from the library, there are many readers there during the darker months, and her colleague was sick. As usual, when the holidays are approaching and the others manage to catch cold, the only fool who is always working and will stand in for any of them is Dagnija. But okay, she lives alone, doesn't need to walk around stores looking for presents, doesn't have to bake cookies . . . Dagnija arrives at Aleksandra's place after dark, finds an open space, parks her car, and goes inside. She rings the doorbell; she still has the keys, but she never uses them.

"Come on in, it's open!" echoes from somewhere deep inside. The question "Dagnija, is that you?" follows when she is already shutting the door behind her.

"Yes, where are you?" she answers as she takes off her boots.

"In the bathroom, you can come in!"

Dagnija opens the door and is overcome with confusion, Aleksandra is sitting in the bathtub, in a fragrant cloud of foam, and in an instant the sight of her dewy breasts tears open the sensory memory of stolen touches, driving all the blood straight into Dagnija's face. She stands there incapable of uttering a word and feels her cheeks and forehead on fire while

69

Aleksandra watches her, and Dagnija is again unsure if it's a smile or smirk stretching across her face.

"I got tired of waiting for you and decided to take a bath," Dagnija's dream woman says as she slides her foamy palm across her shoulder and breast. She's looking Dagnija straight in the eyes. Then she smiles again and slides her palm across her other shoulder and breast . . . "Maybe you'll wash my back? I usually manage on my own, but if you're here, well."

Dagnija's heart leaps out of place and is beating somewhere up around her tonsils, each heartbeat knocking her windpipe shut. Completely dazed, she doesn't know what to say or what to do. Aleksandra's speech and gaze seem smirking, provocative, so Dagnija truly no longer knows if she actually had managed to slip away unnoticed back then . . . If not, then how should she understand Aleksandra's invitation to touch her? Maybe she wants it, maybe Dagnija has been constantly yet needlessly beating down the flame inside herself and now the moment has finally come when she can let it burst forth and melt this damned ice queen. Dagnija doesn't believe it. But she can't fight her desire to touch the skin of her beloved again and so she quietly takes the shower gel and loofah. Gently caressing her, Dagnija alternates between moving the loofah and her palm across the scarred but muscular back. For a long, long time, much longer than she should. She walks her fingers across the nape of Aleksandra's neck, the muscular shoulders hardened from turning the wheelchair, strokes the entire length of her back running the top of her hand over Aleksandra's scars and down to the soft, vulnerable rounds of her buttocks, then along her sides over to her stomach. The loofah has been bobbing in the bubbles for a while now. Aleksandra isn't saying anything either, and Dagnija feels how her body has gradually tensed up under the bubbles. Until finally, flushed and tormented by desire, Dagnija leans down and kisses the tender fold between Aleksandra's shoulder blades.

"What are you doing? Are you nuts, what are you doing?" Aleksandra starts screaming.

Dagnija jerks away and stands up. Then she leans down and tries to cover Aleksandra's mouth with her cupped hand, and, while kissing her at the same time, whispers:

"Don't yell, please, don't yell. I'm not doing anything bad, there's no need to yell."

But Aleksandra doesn't stop.

"Get out of my bathroom, you psycho! Get out of here!"

Dagnija doesn't stop stroking her hair and face, her touch becomes more forceful, while Aleksandra tries to shove away her hands and lips, which keep moving in to kiss one of the available patches of skin.

"Don't yell, please, don't yell, don't do that or I'll have to drown you," Dagnija whispers as if in a trance, "and that spoiled furball of yours right next to you . . ."

Splashes of water in the air, Dagnija kisses Aleksandra's neck behind her ear one more time. Finally, drawing back one of her arms, Aleksandra punches Dagnija right in the eye.

Dagnija howls and jumps to the side . . . She runs out of the bathroom and nearly falls down. Something yowls from under her feet and she, erupting with anger, grabs the meowing, scratching creature, tears open the loggia doors, and throws the animal outside—into the dark. Before shutting the loggia doors

71

again, Dagnija takes a handful snow and forms it into a hard ball. Then she sits down in the living room on the couch and puts the ball on her injured eye . . . The cat tore open her hand, the snow is growing red. As the snow melts, crimson drops slowly roll down her face and fall into her lap. Like bloody tears.

*

Aleksandra is still sitting in the bathtub.

"Perverted bitch! How dare she?"

Anger and shame about the unexpected assault surge across her awareness like hot porridge, but as the water evaporates, her damp skin gradually becomes covered with goosebumps. And maybe not just because it's cold. Aleksandra shudders in disgust remembering Dagnija's lips touching her back. That was the worst of all. After that it was a struggle. A fight. Anger and revulsion suffocate her. Bitch. Before she'd started washing her back, Dagnija had thrown her support loop over the shower rod, and without it Aleksandra can't get out of the bathtub by herself . . . Her phone is also in the back pocket of her wheelchair, but Dagnija had pushed that deep into the bathroom next to the toilet. Aleksandra tries to reach for it, but despite all her efforts, it's no use.

The apartment is quiet, and the outside door hasn't made a sound; it has to be slammed shut pretty forcefully, so Aleksandra knows that Dagnija is still somewhere in the apartment.

Sitting up in the bathtub is getting hard. The water cools off, her wet body is cold. She could lie down, but then all the water would have to be drained. It would be even colder. But if she adds more hot water, then she'll get drowsy. Aleksandra is already shivering and is scared that she will start crying from

72

helplessness. Her back can't support her anymore, any minute now she will end up completely supine. Aleksandra pulls out the drain plug. Who knows what's better—to drown or freeze to death. Supporting herself with her side and elbow against the edge of the bathtub, she decides to give herself over to fate. Whatever will be, will be. After all, there had been times she'd wanted to die. But not today.

*

Dagnija is sitting motionless and thinking about how this is the last time she will visit Aleksandra. She is also thinking about how everything would have been different if she had been able to control her feelings, her desire. Already when Aleksandra had gotten drunk. If only she hadn't given into her desire to touch Aleksandra's body. She would be allowed to be near this goddess for her whole life. Now she's lost everything. It was very difficult to gain Aleksandra's trust. To regain it—probably impossible.

On the wall opposite the couch is a framed watercolor, Dagnija had seen it in the past, but never noticed that the woman in the long dress and tightly combed and braided hair has Aleksandra's profile. Her slender frame is drawn from behind, the outline of her hips swaying in the silvery gray dress and her rounded, girlish shoulders illuminated by pale light, but her face is turned the other way—toward the shadows. Her profile is in semi-darkness, but Dagnija absolutely recognizes Aleksandra's prominent forehead, straight nose, and angled chin. Only her little paunch isn't there yet. Dagnija practically devours the drawing with her eyes. The proportions of Aleksandra's body are different though, now her shoulders are stronger and have muscular definition, while her hips have shrunk and become narrow and weak . . . Dagnija doesn't take her eyes off the drawing for a long time, Aleksandra is so beautiful . . .

A moment later her eyes happened to focus on the clock sitting on the magazine table—forty minutes have already passed since the blowup in the bathroom. Was Aleksandra still soaking in that water? Terrified, Dagnija jumps up and dashes to the bathroom. Aleksandra is lying naked in the empty bathtub, supporting herself against its edge and with a towel thrown over herself; she looks asleep and lightly trembling.

"Aleksandra? Can you hear me?"

Aleksandra opens her eyes and mutters:

"I'm so cold . . ."

Dagnija lowers the support loop but doesn't dare touch her friend.

"Can you get out? Do you have enough strength?"

Aleksandra doesn't even try. She is trembling, and her legs spasm. Dagnija moves the wheelchair closer.

"I'll help you, if you'll let me . . ."

Aleksandra just nods. Taking her under the arms, Dagnija pulls her out of the bathtub, wraps her in a big towel and hugs her tightly in order to slowly sit her down in the wheelchair. Aleksandra's body automatically resists, but she doesn't say anything. Without exchanging a word, they roll to the bedroom, Dagnija puts Aleksandra in a fresh diaper, dresses her in warm pajamas and warm wool socks, and wraps her up as snug as can be.

"Can I stay? Just tonight, still. I'm worried about you, you're so cold."

Aleksandra feels her drenched, chilled flesh burning and sleep slowly overtaking her.

"Where is Ferdinands?" she asks.

Guilt grips Dagnija's breast. She's a villain, a monster. Aleksandra's sweetie—used to warmth and love—was out there somewhere in the neighborhood wandering around in the ice and snow, which is much deeper than he is tall.

"He ran out when I opened the loggia doors," Dagnija lies one last time to Aleksandra. "I'll try calling him, if that doesn't work, I'll go out to look for him. Sleep now, I'll spend the night on the living room couch. Don't be afraid of me, please. I . . . I won't try anything . . ."

Spasms shake Aleksandra's legs from time to time, she is lying quietly and says nothing. Maybe she is already asleep. Dagnija goes out onto the loggia and looks around. The cat is nowhere to be found. She quietly calls its name, but it's no use. She watches the slowly falling flakes indifferently for a moment. Then she goes out into the front room, puts on her boots and coat, and goes outside to look for Ferdinands, though she knows all too well that the cat doesn't trust her and won't come when she calls him.

THE DUCK

He's cute, Laine thinks as she secretly watches the customer sitting at Alīna's desk, and then turns her attention to her monitor again and continues to put together the color palette for the order. Alīna is flirting, coquettishly tilting her head and every so often lowering her eyelids halfway, but she doesn't even realize it. Like always. And always, later on when she's smoking on the balcony, her cheeks red, she curses these stupid men who can't even keep it together long enough to finish a business transaction.

"Gross fucker. Just imagine, he asked me for a pen and practically ripped it out of my hand with my fingers still attached. While I can see a pen right there in his jacket pocket."

She takes another eager drag from her cigarette and puckishly lowers her eyelids.

"But—it's a customer. So, you do it. You smile and do it."

Laine chuckles to herself and gets up to go make another fiendishly strong cup of coffee. This sort of thing doesn't happen to her, she's not as attractive as Alīna and hasn't been as

77

young as her for a long time. Maybe it's better that way, her conversations end up being more matter-of-fact and practical, but when customers walk into the office, they'll always go straight to Alīna without noticing Laine at all.

Laine is not only unattractive, but also objectionably awkward. When she walks past a table where a customer is sitting, she bumps right into the back of his chair with her hip.

"Excuse me," Laine mutters and runs into the office kitchen with her head down.

"Like a duck," she mumbles to herself. She flips on the water kettle and pours five teaspoons of ground coffee into the big cup.

"He's into you," Alīna says to Laine —her eyebrows arched in surprise—when she comes in a moment later as Laine is pouring boiling water into her cup.

"Who are you talking about?" Laine asks in confusion.

"Well, that weird customer, Severīns Whatshisname."

Alīna puts down her cup and throws her spoon into it with a loud clang.

"Haha, I guess that bothers you, huh?" Laine can't help laughing. "You're sick of all those fuckers after all. So, you're actually into them?" she teases her coworker in a friendly way. "How do you know he's into me?"

"Well, he asked for your name and said that maybe he should have you take his order instead. We didn't even end up getting through all the details. What a freak."

Laine smiles to herself. If he doesn't come on to Alīna, then he's a freak, if he does come on to her, then he's a fucker. This chick is totally spoiled when it comes to men.

Laine opens up the cabinet and finds a half-eaten bar of chocolate. That'll do. Everybody has their little indulgences. She breaks off three pieces, stuffs them all into her mouth at the same time, and loudly slurps the hot coffee.

A few days later, Severīns is back and heads straight for Laine.

"Hi, Laine!" He comes up too close, looks her straight in the eyes, then stretches out his hand to greet her.

Laine is not used to this sort of familiarity, she wants to giggle, even more so because she can see Alīna's pretty face rolling her eyes behind the man's back.

Severīns is looking for the cheapest graphic design package for his company.

"The cheapest package from the cheapest shop," Laine thinks to herself without a hint of loyalty to her workplace.

But they are able to reach an agreement, Laine is practical and doesn't waste time on batting her eyelids or smiling flirtatiously. She isn't attractive enough for that kind of fooling around to suit her.

Up close, Laine also finds Severīns attractive. Slender, dark hair, brown eyes, with well-groomed hands, perfectly pleated pants, and a flawless knot in his tie. It's a bit strange though how he doesn't smile at all. The corners of his mouth occasionally jerk to one side, but the resulting grimace bears only a distant resemblance to a smile.

"We could go somewhere and have some tea," he says at their last meeting after his order is ready.

The unexpected offer leaves Laine practically speechless.

"Sure. Right now?" That's all she manages to say.

"Well, yeah, why not?"

Laine walks into the break room, gives herself a look in the mirror. She uses her hands to fluff up her curly, always out of control hair. She decides that it might be time to start using eyeliner again—her look has gotten really basic and plain. Then she puts on her coat and is ready to go.

Right on the corner is a bakery—you can buy fresh pastries and have a coffee, tea, or juice. Visions of one of their crispy, cream-filled twists were already dancing before her eyes, but without asking, Severīns orders them both peppermint tea, and then they sit, waiting for their scalding drinks to cool down a little.

"You're single, right?" he asks, cutting straight to the point. Laine even recoils a bit from the frankness.

"Well, yeah . . . The kids are grown up, out of the house. But I've got a cat," she laughs.

Severīns doesn't.

"Me too, I'm unattached right now. Maybe we could meet again sometime?" he asks. Laine looks at this pleasant man sitting across from her and can't tell if she likes his directness or not. But she's been single for so long that maybe it's just worth giving it a shot? Her husband left her ten years ago and since then it's never really worked out . . . If it doesn't work this time either, then she can go on living like she has up until now—but if it works?

Severīns notices Laine's long stare and his lips jerk to the side again. That must be how he truly smiles; Laine likes it better when he doesn't.

They don't go to cafes anymore. Severīns suggests they go for a walk, and the next few times they meet, they chat pleasantly as they wander around the Ķengarags Promenade, which is right by Laine's home. Severīns talks a lot, but afterward Laine can never really remember what he said. Something about computers, history, corrupt politics, and the dimwittedness of society . . . Boring, but Laine smiles politely and every so often asks him to repeat something. The path is covered with yellow leaves, Laine delights in deeply inhaling the smell of autumn. A couple comes toward them who are about their age—a little under fifty—and clearly with eyes only for each other. The man holds the woman tightly around her waist, roses the color of sunset tremble in her hands. Their faces nose-to-nose, they're quietly and gently chatting, just like teenagers.

"You like flowers?" Severīns suddenly asks.

Laine smiles and wants to say—what woman doesn't like them . . . But she doesn't get the chance.

"Totally pointless weeds. You put them in a vase and three days later they stink and have to be thrown out," he continues.

"I like them," Laine feels a little annoyed, but still speaks up. Severīns shoots her a mocking glance, and his mouth jerks to one side again.

"To hell with him. Creep. I don't need somebody like that," Laine thinks to herself, but Severīns grabs her around the shoulders, pulls her closer to him, and presses his lips awkwardly to her temples.

It feels warm. Laine likes it.

"You and those weeds. I'll marry you and buy you a house and a car. Or whatever else you want."

He kisses Laine again. This time on the lips. He knows how to kiss . . .

"Will you be mine?"

It turns out that Severīns is a great cook. On his first visit, he shows up at Laine's fifth-floor apartment with a salad, fresh greens, goat cheese, and all kinds of other goodies. Also, a bunch of something, perhaps basil, he hands it to Laine like a bouquet and kisses her, his mouth jerking to one side again, but Laine feels a little offended. If he's not bringing her flowers, then fine, but why joke around like that. But then he drives Laine out of the kitchen, and twenty minutes later he brings out a fresh, luscious, fantastically fragrant and delicious salad. And an unusual, but very aromatic tea—supposedly a twenty-four-herb blend.

"Well, what do you think?" he asks, clearly expecting praise.

"Amazing!" Laine answers, and she's not lying.

"You probably don't cook anything at home. I didn't find anything sensible in your fridge or shelves." Severīns concludes.

"I hate cooking, usually I eat in town or order a pizza," Laine admits honestly.

"What a waste. A woman should be thriftier."

He gives that maybe smile again.

Laine is a little ashamed of her dirty gas stove, which she only rarely uses, and also about the cat hair on the couch and armchair. There's no sign of Mika—strange, usually, if someone shows up, her cat is there right away, he doesn't climb up onto anyone, but gets comfortable someplace where he can keep an eye on everything, and lounges around, showing off his gorgeous sandy coat. What a cutie. Laine's friend on lonely nights and the apple of her eye, going on eleven years.

"I can offer you wine or brandy," she says suddenly snapping back and getting up from the couch.

"I don't drink!" Severīns suddenly sounds stern.

"Okay, fine," she answers calmly. "But I'm going to pour myself a glass."

"I'd really appreciate it if you could manage without alcohol around me . . ."

"Interesting," Laine thinks and stops in the middle of room. "Who is he to tell me what I can and can't do?"

After hesitating for a moment, Laine sits back down on the couch. It would be silly for her to sit there sipping wine on her own. She'll have a glass of Riesling when he's gone.

Severīns moves from the armchair next to her on the couch. Laine doesn't know how to act, she feels so big and awkward, but Severīns takes his hot palm and turns her face toward him and kisses her lips, neck, ear. Laine feels herself grow warm, but thinks, not yet, she doesn't want to sleep with this man yet. She doesn't really know anything about him, they've only known each other for three weeks. Laine isn't sure they need to and, goddammit, why is she trying to convince herself that she needs a reason not to. She just doesn't want to!

Severīns has stuck his hand under her loose tunic and is already stroking Laine's stomach. She shoves away his pushy hand.

"No, Severīns, not yet. Don't."

But he's stronger.

"But you want to, stop . . . don't pretend.

With his other hand he's undone Laine's bra, her large, warm breasts resting in his palm, which is already grasping at them, her nipples are erect and hard. Severīns takes one of them in his fingers and gently pinches it.

"You can lie, but these don't. You want to."

Laine doesn't want to. She really doesn't and now she's forcing back Severīns's powerful hands, but she's just not strong enough. Struggling against Laine's resistance, he's managed to take off not only all of her clothes, but also all of his, and now they're both naked, struggling against each other on the couch.

"Severīns, please! No. I don't want to, do you hear me?"

She presses her thighs together tightly and is using her hands to rebuff Severīns's attempts to pry them apart. Her skin chafes against the rough fabric of the couch until she understands that there's no sense in resisting. She just isn't strong enough. And then she lets Severīns do what he wants. It doesn't take long. And it doesn't hurt. After he finishes, he slumps down next to her and stares at her naked body. And then smacks her stomach with his palm. It quivers.

"If you lost a dozen kilograms or so, you'd be perfect. I can meal plan for you if you want."

Laine doesn't say anything. She thinks about how she really, really needs to take a shower, but how would it look if she walked naked to the bathroom now . . . Laine gets up and goes anyway, but feels Severīns's stare on her full bottom and the fatty folds under her shoulder blades.

"I'm not going to see him anymore," Laine thinks as she rinses off in the lukewarm shower. "Just another man, just another fucker, like Alīna would say, and I don't want him."

Laine's life is fine without any men in it; plus, she is not thrifty enough and too fat.

She dries off and wraps the towel around herself before heading back to the room. Severīns isn't dressed yet and puts something quickly back on the table. He notices that Laine sees this, and he calmly explains:

"I bumped your phone and it almost fell on the ground. I just barely caught it."

Laine takes the phone and flips it open. An unanswered call—Pūks.

"My sister called," she says.

"What's your sister's name?" Severīns wants to know.

"Beāte," Laine answers.

"Really, just like my wife? Ex-wife, of course."

Severīns sounds skeptical, but this is the first time that he's mentioned his wife.

Laine thinks that she prefers him being divorced instead of being a permanent bachelor.

"Do you have any kids?" she asks.

A new expression washes across Severīns's face, one Laine hadn't seen yet. That same smile or smirk, but his mouth is open and its corners are stretched even more than usual. As if he were baring his teeth.

"I've got an eleven-year-old son." Severīns answers with a smirk. "Who I haven't seen in a year and a half and don't even know where he is. Some broads don't get that a boy needs his father."

Laine starts feeling a little sorry for Severīns. He misses his boy and is angry about their separation. Maybe that explains his sullenness. That's understandable.

"If I knew where they were and had a gun, I'd just shoot that bitch."

He's still smirking. Laine can't tell if he's joking or being serious, but she doesn't like this at all anymore. Severīns comes up and hugs her again. Standing so close to her, Laine can smell what happened a moment ago—their bodily excretions are still drying on his body and the scent is nauseating.

"Give me a clean towel, I want to wash off," Severīns says. Laine goes into the other room and finds a clean, but slightly crumpled towel. Mika looks sullen as he sits on the windowsill staring out the window. Laine smiles at the cat, "Jealous, huh?"

Severīns gets in the shower. As soon as she hears the water turn on, Laine's phone rings again. From the ringtone she can tell that it's one of her children, there's still some time until Severīns will be out of the bathroom, and Laine answers the phone. Her daughter. She wants to talk, because she's got some boy trouble, but Laine isn't ready for that kind of a conversation right now.

"Krista, I'll call you back in about an hour, okay?"

But Krista ignores this and just keeps talking, and Laine repeats again that she doesn't have time right now.

"I don't matter to you at all?" her daughter asks discontentedly.

The shower shuts off and Laine doesn't want to talk to her child in Severīns's presence.

"I'm sorry, I can't talk right now. I'll call you later, okay? Kisses."

He comes out of the shower still naked and quietly gets dressed. He picks up each piece of clothing off the floor one at a time, first forcefully shaking it, brushing it off with his hand, and only then putting it on. Laine is sitting still wrapped in her towel. Waiting for him to finally leave. She doesn't want a man in her life. She doesn't like Severīns. She's not bothered by the dirty stove, the cat hair, or her own extra kilograms. She's bothered by this strange man.

"Who was that one the phone?" Severīns asks as he buttons his shirt.

"My daughter. But does it matter?"

He carefully buttons his shirt cuffs and comes to stand very close to Laine. He puts his palm against the side of her neck under her disheveled hair and pulls her head to his chest. Tightly. Too tightly. His fingers are hard and dig painfully into her neck. Laine's nose is pushed into Severīns's chest muscles, his shirt just barely smells of laundry detergent, and it's difficult for her to breathe.

"Don't ever lie to me," he whispers.

Him whispering those words sounds scarier than if he'd yelled them. Laine says nothing. She's frightened and waiting for Severīns to walk out the door.

Three days go by. Severīns sends her a text: "Hi. Let's meet tonight after work?"

Laine slumps down. She had hoped that it was all over, that he wouldn't text her anymore, or call, or invite her out. After all, she's too fat, too awkward, and doesn't know how to cook. Remembering his visit makes her feel dirty—and not because of the oven or cat hair.

Laine is at work and doesn't answer right away. Ten minutes later Severīns calls. For a moment she thinks whether to answer it or not. Then she walks into the office kitchen and presses the talk button.

"Yes, Severīns."

"Hi! I sent you a text."

"Yes, hi, I saw."

"Why didn't you answer? Should we meet tonight? I've been aching to squeeze those big breasts of yours and dive into your depths. It was perfect, right?"

Laine feels a shudder run down her throat as it clenches. She needs some water.

"Why aren't you saying anything? What time are we meeting?"

"I don't think I can tonight."

"How come?"

"My daughter said she would come over, she needs to talk," Laine lies.

"But she's not going to stay the night, right? I could come later."

"I don't know. I don't think we should."

"Stop it. Last time you also said we shouldn't, but it turned out to be so good."

Laine is absolutely sure that she doesn't want to.

"Severīns, I don't want to. I don't think we should see each other," she gathers up her courage and pushes it all out in one breath.

"What, are you crazy? Is there somebody else? Is it Pūks, the one you were giving kisses to on the phone?" Severīns's voice has an unmistakably mocking tone.

"Pūks is my sister, I've called her that since we were kids."

Laine doesn't even understand why she's explaining herself, she wants to end the conversation, but is too polite to do it.

She's waiting for Severīns to hear, to understand, and accept that they won't be seeing each other again.

"What happened? Everything was so perfect. What else does the princess on the pea want? You want flowers? I'll buy you an armful of red roses, you must miss those weeds." She can hear the same mocking tone in his voice again.

"I said all I've got to say. I'm sorry."

Laine ends the call.

Laine is the last one at the office, everyone here works on a pretty open schedule. The main thing is not to be late fulfilling an order, but nobody tracks how many hours you spend here, when you arrive, or when you leave. After checking that all the windows are tightly closed and turning off all the lights, Laine punches in the security code by the exit and walks out. She has twenty seconds to engage all four locks. She never likes this moment when she's standing in a small, illuminated spot by the main door and can't see what's happening behind her as she's locking up. There—in the dark. That never feels comfortable.

But, as always, everything ends up being fine. Except that when she goes to stick the keys into her bag, the whole bunch slides past and falls with a clatter on the ground. Laine grumbles to herself:

"Always a klutz!" and leans down to pick up the keys. And that's it. Just the tram and then home.

The street isn't very well lit, the last leaves on the tree branches are still obscuring the yellowish glow of the streetlights. Laine is used to it and knows every bump on this sidewalk. Somebody's behind her. Really close, but doesn't pass her. Laine isn't scared, but she doesn't like it. She speeds up. The person behind her keeps pace. Laine stops a moment later, pretending to look for something in her purse. Her companion also stops. Laine is afraid to look back, she doesn't know what the stranger has in mind. She shoves her purse under her arm and starts running toward the tram stop. It's not far. But as she runs, she no longer hears what's happening behind her. There's an illuminated patch up ahead and two boys are chatting as they walk toward her. Laine runs past them and then stops and looks back. It's hard to see down the dim street, but it seems like nobody's there.

Laine is out of breath by the time she reaches the stop, and the tram arrives straight away. She keeps looking back to make sure nobody is following her, but she was the last to arrive at the stop and, aside from her, only an older couple and a young girl with a backpack got on.

As the tram pulls away, her breathing slows. Laine thinks maybe someone was just fooling with her. They didn't do anything, they didn't even touch her. She gets off at the Prūši Street stop and sets off toward home at a brisk pace, but she still feels off, even though this time nobody is following her. Quickly up the stairs, into the apartment, and she's there. That's it, everything's okay. It's warm at home and a very sleepy Mika trundles out from the living room. Laine leans down to ruffle her sweetie's fur.

Her phone dings, she's gotten a text. Laine slips off her coat, takes the phone out of her purse, and reads the message: "Hi, princess! I can't get our last date out of my mind, you were so hot and wild. Let's meet tomorrow night? Kisses."

Laine shudders. Severīns hadn't written her since their last phone call, which was a week and a half ago. She'd been sure that he'd gotten the message and moved on . . . She doesn't know what to do—should she answer or just ignore him. And she starts wondering if maybe it had been Severīns following her down that dark street. She ruffles her hair and turns her head, relaxing her neck. Her throat still recalls the grip of Severīns's hard fingers. She decides to answer: "No, Severīns. I already said everything there was to say."

Her cat is cuddling up closer to her than usual. Every so often he lets out an inquisitive meow. Laine puts Mika in her lap as she sits down, and thinks. The cat snuggles up to her breasts and rubs one of his ears against her hand as he purrs. Severīns doesn't write her again.

It's Friday. Laine feels a little nervous all day long. The phone rings and she practically jumps. It's Pūks. Her sister invites her to stop by after work for a glass of wine, and Laine is happy. They'll chat, time will go by without them noticing it. If she's lucky, her sister's guy will drive her home.

Her guy, Laine chuckles to herself, but that's exactly what Pūks calls her tall, athletic, well-mannered husband who climbs mountains and kayaks down rapid-filled rivers. Pūks got lucky. That doesn't happen to everybody . . . Laine laughs again.

Her evening is saved; this time Laine doesn't leave last, she and Alīna leave together, and Uģis—the designer—is still slaving over the calendar proofs. As she walks with Alīna, Laine keeps looking around, the street is already dark before five in November, but she doesn't see anybody. This time they're also heading in the same direction on the tram, Laine is visiting her sister, and at this hour there are so many people at the stop that it's impossible to take them all in at a glance . . . But this time Laine feels safe.

She has fun at her sister's. They each have two glasses of wine, talk about Laine's daughter's troubles, about her sister's "guy's" last trip to the Caucasus, about their health, about her sister's new dress. Her sister is two years older and as amply proportioned as Laine, but her "guy" has been with her since their early youth and in spite of many storms, high tides and low, they haven't considered divorce even once. Laine is happy, but also a bit jealous. Not everybody gets that . . . Severīns and all of the worries that have brought her down are on the tip of Laine's tongue, but Laine feels uncomfortable telling her sister that she slept with a nearly complete stranger. Her sister considers Laine to be practically a nun and she isn't totally wrong. To tell her how she didn't want to, but that Severīns forced her, seems even stupider. Laine keeps quiet. Her sister's opinion of her matters.

Her sister's guy takes her home, right to her front door, of course, and even asks if she wants him to walk with her upstairs. Laine has had two glasses of wine and isn't scared. She's not really ever scared, except lately on occasion . . . Laine says goodbye and walks into the stairwell. The light switch doesn't work. Feeling her way around, she makes her way up to the second floor, but there's no light there either. She climbs and climbs, and there's no light all the way to the top—the fifth floor. She can't help but feel scared. Laine stops at the landing before the last half-floor and pulls out her phone to light up the space by her front door. There's nobody there. Her neighbors in the apartment opposite are away, they show up twice a year, so if anything bad happens, there's no reason even to try pounding on their door . . . She finds her keys using her phone's light, then sticks her phone back in her purse and walks up the last steps. She feels around with her fingers and finds the keyhole, and her door is open when suddenly something largeish, furry, and moist falls down from above, hits her head, slides down her face, and falls on the ground. Laine can't tell what it was, but trips over it, dashes inside her apartment, slams the door, and with her hands shaking, turns the top and bottom locks and puts up the chain. Then she turns on the light and sees herself in the mirror. Her whole forehead is covered in blood . . .

"Mika, Mika!" she yells and runs around her apartment, turning on all the lights and lamps.

She can't find Mika, Laine is panicking, but then she sees her cat sitting hunched in the corner by the radiator. He looks scared but is fine. Laine is crying and wants to pick him up and hug him, but the creature hisses and bats at her with his paw, and then Laine remembers her bloody face. She runs into the bathroom and scrubs her forehead, washes her face, finally gets into the shower, rinses off her entire body, and also washes her hair. "What was that, what was that," she keeps repeating to herself, but can't gin up the courage to go and look—what was it? Maybe she should call Pūks, so her guy could come back and take a look, he might be only halfway home by now. Laine walks to the door, presses her ear up to it, and listens carefully. There's nothing there. Not a single sound, only the usual evening murmurs floating up from the apartments below. It'll be okay, she thinks. A moment later she listens again, then pours herself another glass of wine, turns off the lights, and sits in the dark sipping her cool drink. Mika sits down next to her, snuggles up to her hip, and falls asleep.

There's a dead duck lying in the stairwell. A wild duck, probably from right around here by the Daugava . . . With broken legs, its stomach cut open, decapitated—it doesn't so much look like it was cut off as ripped off. Laine looks up but can't understand how and from where the duck fell on her last night. And how did it get there? Severīns? Laine isn't sure and is a little annoyed with herself that she's blaming everything unexplainable and frightening on him. But nothing like that ever used to happen . . . She finds a trash bag, sticks her hand into a smaller bag and, taking it by its broken legs, cleans up the duck. She takes it out to the bin, then climbs back up and uses a wet rag to wipe off all the spots of blood on the door jamb and concrete floor. Everything is clean now.

On Monday at work, Laine is even more anxious and scatter-brained than before. She jumps at practically every unexpected noise. Alīna watches her on the sly until finally asking:

"Hey, are you okay? Did something happen?"

"No, no, everything's okay," Laine answers, considering for a moment whether to tell Alīna about the duck, but that would only prompt more questions and it's pretty clear that Laine should keep Alīna from guessing, otherwise she'll have to talk about her romance with a customer.

No, everything is fine. Laine pulls herself together and gets to work.

Nothing else happens. Nobody chases Laine down the street, nobody leaves animal corpses in her apartment, nobody sends her texts asking to see her.

A week has gone by, it's Friday night. Laine comes home after work and the lights are off in the stairwell again. She pulls out her phone and holds it in her hand. But doesn't flip it open. She climbs up slowly, stopping every so often to listen. Silence. She keeps climbing until the last half-floor and stops. Silence. Laine turns the display toward her door and flips it open. Nothing. Nobody. She keeps climbing and illuminates every corner and door jamb with her phone's light.

"There's nothing there. I'm becoming stupidly paranoid." Laine thinks, unlocks the door, dashes inside as if she were running from somebody, and carefully turns each lock.

Severīns stops writing her. Laine gradually calms down, lets go, and thinks maybe she'd been unfair by blaming all those odd occurrences on him. Some kind of weird coincidence. The strange events gradually fade from her recollection—did it all really happen that way? Laine isn't putting up the chain every night anymore and only locks the main—bottom—lock.

Laine has arrived home from her daughter's place, it's late, almost midnight, and she starts climbing up the stairs. The stairwell light is on, and Laine doesn't lift her eyes, just keeps climbing. And after the final turn she raises her head and sees Severīns standing by her apartment door. He's resting his shoulder against the wall, his lips are pulled to one side just like when he was talking about his ex-wife, but he's holding roses. Ten or twelve, maybe fifteen. Laine stops.

"I've been waiting for you for so long, where were you? Are you seeing somebody?" he asks.

Laine is tired, confused, she'd like to run back downstairs, but where would she go? To call for help? Wake up one of her neighbors, and then what would she say? That there was a man standing by her door with roses?

She climbs up and says to him:

"What do you want? What do you really want?"

Severīns's lips are still pulled to one side as he hands Laine the roses and says:

"You're mine, we agreed, don't you remember."

Laine doesn't remember that they'd talked about anything of the sort. She doesn't take the roses being thrust toward her, but stands without saying a word, and Severīns seems to misunderstand. He comes closer and grabs her with the arm holding the roses, but with his other arm shoves Laine against the wall, forcefully, painfully squeezing her breasts and pawing at her groin. Laine resists and fights back. She fights by hissing and spitting, pushing him off of her with her hands and knees, their scuffle echoing all the way down the stairwell. Mika starts meowing behind the door. Somewhere further down she hears someone open their inner door, they must be listening, and the two of them quiet down. Laine feels ashamed, and she sees no way out . . .

"Let's go inside," Severīns whispers.

"No," Laine says. "No," she repeats.

"Then I'll take you right here," he whispers, and his lips jerk to one side again. "You'll like it, you'll see. Just like last time."

"Get off of me!" now Laine is shouting, but in a whispered voice.

"Dumb bitch, you're really starting to get on my nerves. Oh, look, the princess is here. You're a duck, a fat, stupid duck, not a princess." He says the last sentence in his regular speaking voice.

Laine panics, the blood drains from her head, and she feels slightly dizzy, remembers the crippled, headless body of the duck. It was lying right here, right in this spot . . .

A door opens downstairs again, this time both doors—also the outer one. Nobody comes out into the stairwell, but they must be listening carefully. Then the door closes again.

"If you don't leave right now, I'll scream," Laine whispers. "I'll scream for the police."

Severīns grips her wrist tightly and twists it. Laine groans in pain. Behind the door, Mika is meowing again and now also scratching. In the dark, empty stairwell, it's all too loud.

"Fine," he goes back to whispering. "I'll go, but you know that I know where you work, I know where you live. Think it over carefully. And I like you even though you're too fat and lazy. I've got no idea what's so irresistible about you . . ."

He squeezes Laine's wrist one more time, takes the bunch of roses and shoves their ends into her coat pocket, and then heads quietly, on tiptoe, down the stairs. None of the doors open again on the lower floors . . .

The fresh-faced officer on duty is attentive. Laine has to explain what happened, why she'd come to the station, and then they'll write the report together. Laine talks but feels ashamed, she'd let a strange man break into her life and home, she doesn't understand how it could've happened, and why she can't handle it on her own. But she keeps talking. About everything. No—almost everything. And about how she's afraid. The police officer thinks she needs to petition the court for a restraining order. Laine doesn't understand.

"He won't be allowed to come near you," the police officer says.

"I don't know if he's really threatening me . . ." Laine feels confused. "I don't want to exaggerate."

The officer asks questions and writes down Laine's personal information. She rattles it off all in order. The person who'd threatened her: First name, last name. ID number?

"I don't know," Laine answers.

Home address?

"I don't know . . . I could find his address at work."

"Phone number? What's the nature of your relationship?" The officer gives several options: "Husband, shared household, do you have any children together?" Laine shakes her head.

"No, no."

"Some other kind of relationship? What kind?"

Laine doesn't know what to say.

"Have you had an intimate relationship with the person threatening you?"

Laine blushes and whispers: "Yes."

"Consensually?"

"Well, I'm not sure, maybe . . ."

"Can anyone testify or is there any other evidence of his threatening behavior? Correspondence? Photographs? Witnesses? A statement from a doctor?"

Laine doesn't say anything. There's nothing. Maybe it's not like she felt, like she thought? But it was all there—he forced himself on her, the bloody duck had been real, and the flesh of her neck and wrist still recalled his painful touch.

Laine repeats it all to the police officer again, but this time tells him everything, also the things she'd kept silent about earlier—the humiliating struggle on the couch, the person following her in the dark, the bloody duck by her door. The police officer listens and the whole time keeps writing things down. When she's finished, he asks Laine to read and sign it. Laine stares at the completed form for a moment but can't seem to concentrate and read what's written there, just signs. Meanwhile the police officer is typing something on the computer.

"Maybe I don't need to, maybe . . ."

Laine wants to say that she's not completely sure, "Maybe the person following me that night and the duck had nothing to do with Severīns . . ." But the police officer interrupts her:

"No, you should. You did the right thing coming here . . . Definitely the right thing. This person is in the database, and two years ago he was subject to an immediate restraining order. You got off much easier . . ."

"You just have to wait for the court ruling, but I don't think that there will be any problems with that," the police officer says.

Laine goes home and thinks that maybe she should move. Find a new apartment somewhere closer to her sister; in terms of price, her Ķengarags apartment will probably be worth less, but one bedroom is enough for Laine. For Laine and Mika.

Laine didn't go to work today since she went to the police. It's the middle of the day, and pale, slanted December sunshine fills the sky, and Laine feels utterly tired and hopeless. She climbs up to the fifth floor, she's scared, and doesn't know if her fear will ever go away. She goes into her apartment, carefully locks everything behind her, and puts up the chain. Mika is spread across the windowsill catching the rays of the stingy winter sunshine, which heats the room through the window for a few hours. Laine can't keep her eyes open, she takes a blanket, lies down on the couch, and is asleep in an instant.

She wakes with a start in total darkness. Mika has moved next to her and is quietly snoring. Laine stretches out her hand to turn on the light, but it doesn't react. The bulb probably burned out. Laine feels worry starting to eat away at her, but she tries to calm herself down. Feeling her way around she makes her way to the light switch, but the lights don't come on. Laine listens, the fridge in the kitchen is also quiet . . . Without making a sound, in just her socks, she walks over to her apartment's outer door. She stands and listens. Her heart is pounding and the blood rushing through her ears so loudly that she can't hear anything. She suddenly feels soft fur rubbing against her feet, a purring Mika meows. There's a sound outside too, as if someone just ran their palm across the door. Laine feels around for her purse without success, that's where her phone is. She just needs to remember where she put it when she came in . . .

"You hear me, don't you?" Severīns whispers through the gap by the door. "Let me in, we need to talk."

Laine doesn't say a word and keeps looking for her purse.

"I haven't even done anything to you. Why did you push me away? It all started out great, what happened? Please, let me in, let's talk. I love you."

Laine hears the door handle jiggling up and down, but the door is locked with both keys, and the chain is up. She finally finds her purse, it's on the table in the kitchen.

No, Laine isn't all that tidy and doesn't always put things down where they should be.

She goes to the farthest—smallest—room, closes the door, and for the first time in her life calls the police.

"Someone is trying to break into my apartment . . . No, I don't know who . . . They've shut off the power . . . Yes, my address is . . . please, come quick . . . I'm scared . . ."

Then she sits down on the floor and listens as Severīns keeps whispering and whispering to her. She can't make out the words. Then he starts wrenching the door handle with more force. He struggles with it for a moment, then stops. It's quiet for a while, and then Laine smells smoke, at first only barely, but then she feels the smoke gradually getting stronger, thickening, she wants to shut Mika into the room farthest from the door, but he is hiding somewhere and doesn't respond to her quietly calling his name.

Laine uses her phone light to find a bucket, fills it with water and splashes it onto the inside of the door. The stream of smoke lessens for a moment, but then picks up strength again. She can hear Severīns's muffled laughter in the stairwell and him coughing every so often.

Laine hears people coming up from below. Several of them. Determined, strong steps. She wets the towel, puts it over her mouth, and waits.

THE BEST TIME OF YOUR LIFE

"Don't hide," I whisper without turning my head. "I can't see you anyway."

He doesn't move. His shadow is still falling across my back and the early midday sun warms only the rounded contour of my left shoulder blade and hip and the shiny, flushed skin above my bikini bottom.

Behind the dunes there's the muffled sound of crashing waves, but around me sedge, stonecrop, and baby's breath shimmer and exude a nauseating honeyed scent. Hot sand and warm, still air in the hollow between the dunes. Every so often a large fly or a small horsefly, I'm not sure which, buzzes by; if they start to land on me, I'll probably move to the side of the dunes facing the sea, where it's a bit breezy with far fewer bugs. But they don't land on me.

It's sweltering.

He's still standing behind me. I'm sitting on a towel in lotus position with my legs crossed, eyes closed, nostrils flared, and slowly, deliberately drawing air in through them, trying to catch the scent of his skin, its excretions, the sweat of his armpits and groin, his deodorant, shaving cream, anything . . . Sometimes it works, but this time the baby's breath is overwhelming everything around it.

"Why aren't you saying anything?" I ask. "You haven't come here in a long time."

Swollen and sun-chapped lips, I lick them with my nearly dry tongue. Salty. A few grains of sand remain in my mouth. I rub them against the roof of my mouth with the tip of my tongue, but don't spit them out. Spitting would wrench me out of this trance-like state. I don't know if I want that.

He's moved. The sun is no longer baking my shoulder and hip. He's come closer or taken a step to the side. I'm thirsty. Somewhere off to the right of me there's a water bottle in the sand. I don't reach for it and still don't open my eyes.

Silence. Sea. Sand. I feel a drop of sweat as it takes a meandering path, stopping at times, and slides from my shoulder blades down my back. Nearly all the way to my bikini bottom. Sand crunching underfoot, a hot finger catches the drop, and a rough fingertip traces its path across my back as it slides up to my shoulder blades. I don't open my eyes. There's thundering in my ears and I feel pinpricks on the skin across my whole body as if it had been scorched from fine little sparks of sand.

I reach for the water and open my eyes. The world is much brighter than I'd expected, my eyes are dazzled, watering, feeling around I unscrew the bottle, rinse my mouth, take a sip, and smear my wet palms across my face.

Only then do I look back. There's nobody there. "Hey," I call out quietly, "hey!"

I cast a glance across the top of the dunes, at the path through the willows; there's nobody there. Just the goosebumps on my stomach and forearms, but those gradually disappear too in the hot sun.

Valts is rocking angrily on the soles of both feet from the tips of his toes to his heels and back again. His arms crossed across his chest. Some kind of indie music is coming from the speakers, he walks over, turns it down, but doesn't shut it off. He crosses his arms and starts rocking again, completely out of sync with the beat of the music.

"Do you even know what that woman's name is?"

"Ingrīda," I answer calmly. My head hurts.

"Ingrīda—who?"

"Ingrīda—the shop owner. Settle down, it's all arranged, I trust her."

"Trust her. You don't even know her last name."

Valts walks up to the boxes, each of which contains an organza sachet of stone jewelry. Arons already took half of them to Riga this morning. Valts takes one of the sachets and pulls a bracelet out of it. Thin red and white leather straps, a flat beach stone, black with white veining, and a tiny white crystal set in it. I'm looking at Valts's shoulders, his brawny neck—tanned red-brown—visible under his shirt. His hair bleached by the summer sun. Someone is pounding out a precise beat with a hammer on the inside of my head.

Ingrīda went nuts when she saw my jewelry around Arons's wife's neck and wrist. She needs ones exactly like that in her shop. She called and I was so excited that I agreed right away.

105

"Valts, if it all just keeps sitting around here, it's not doing anyone any good anyway."

"It's not about doing anyone any good. But about this endless naivete . . . You're having somebody you barely know take it all to some woman you don't know and about who you know nothing at all—her address, her last name, not even if it's actually her real name."

"Let it go. Somebody will buy it, somebody will like it."

"And somebody will take advantage of you." Valts uses his tone to make it clear that the conversation is over. "Whatever, I'm going to work, give it some more thought."

Then he's gone. The headache doesn't feel like pounding hammers anymore, but is now a constant pressure that doesn't relent. I take the bracelet Valts had pulled out and tie it around my wrist. I lift my hand above my head and watch it for a long time. Then I turn off the music.

I always work in silence, I like to hear everything happening around me, in the house, in the yard, behind the fence. Every rustle, swish, creak, bang, pant, knock, drip, and drum . . . I open my email, I've received something. I download the file and go into the kitchen to make some coffee, deadly strong, so it knocks me over the head, maybe the pain will go away.

I stir the coffee so the grounds settle faster, and get to work. My head hurts so much that I'm afraid to lean down, I'm sitting with my back straight and reading the description sent to me. I don't understand a thing, I read it again, and once more after that. The open window creaks, a late blooming jasmine branch knocks against the glass and scrapes against it. The wind is kicking up, maybe it'll finally summon up some rain.

I can't. I'm not able to work, I leave the document open and go into the other room to lie down for a moment. I put my head on the pillow and close my eyes.

He comes up quietly and sits down by my feet. He doesn't touch me, but I feel the mattress sag from his weight, and my feet turn at a slightly awkward angle, so I cross them one over the other and get more comfortable.

"You can't cope with life," he says. "You naively believe everyone except yourself."

"I don't believe you either anymore," I whisper spitefully.

He puts his hand on my knee, then lays his entire body across my legs and presses his face into my stomach. I feel how he slowly breathes hot breath through my thin skirt, my skin feels like it's searing. It's hot enough already and so I quickly push him off of me. I get up from the bed, only then opening my eyes and, without looking back, I take off. I run through both rooms, past the kitchen, I stick my feet in my slippers, then cross the yard, and then am already on the street. I carefully close the gate. Hanging my arm over the fence I feel around and shove the bolt shut.

The wind is tugging and whipping my thin house dress and flinging my hair into my eyes. The sky is completely clear, blue, cloudless. The heat isn't as oppressive anymore and so I keep walking down the gravel road. There's no sidewalk where there should be one; instead there's a path worn by footsteps, separated from the road in places by yellowing tufts of grass, a roadside rosette, and some artemisia stalks, but in other spots there's only a low gravel berm undisturbed by cars and untrampled by feet. I move quickly, at times so fast to the point that

I'm practically running. "Yes, you need to run away, there's no other option," he says right in my ear.

I spin around and scream at him: "Fuck off! Get out of here, you jerk! I know what to do!" The sun is pressing down from above onto my aching head. A woman with a dog on the other side of the street stops and watches me carefully. She looks one way, then the other. The dog doesn't care, a plump dachshund, sniffing the tufts of grass, he trots along and pulls the woman with him. I know that the dachshund's owner doesn't see who I'm talking to. The same as me. The dog drags the woman on, she looks back a couple of times, but I don't move.

"You don't know anything. You don't even know where you're going right now or why," he says in a mocking tone.

I turn around and continue confidently walking forward. On the right side of the street, the line of private homes ends and the coastal thicket begins—tiny pines growing askew, sea buckthorn, willows. I turn down a sandy path and head deeper into the underbrush. My feet sink into the sand, my ankles are wobbly in my unsteady slippers so I take them off and hold them in my hand. The willow switches whip my legs and face, my dress tangles in branches and around my feet. Yes, I'm running way, I'm afraid, I can't stop, the dune keeps getting higher and I scramble up onto it, pressing my palms down into the sand for support, I scramble right up to the top and then plunge down the other side, the slope on the descent is too steep, I trip over my own feet and tumble headlong to the bottom.

I sit up and look around. Ten, a hundred, a thousand pairs of eyes are watching me, the beach is filled with half-naked flesh. Everyone is silent and frozen and staring right at me. I can't stand it, my head hurts, but I don't scream and instead I close my eyes.

"See, they're all looking," he says. "They're looking and laughing at you, you awkward bitch."

I can sense the proportions of his body and his movements only through my closed eyes. Right now, he's sitting next to me, I hear the sound of trickling sand. He's probably grabbing a handful and letting the individual grains slip through the gaps between his fingers back down onto the ground. He does it again and again. The sound of the sand calms me a bit. I pull my knees up to my chest and grip my head with my hands so I'm not visible, so that the thousands of eyes turn away and gape again at each other's bare flesh, at each other's bodies— thin or housed in fat folds, pink, sweaty, oily, overroasted, and exuding a cloyingly sweet, sour, sickening stench.

"That won't help. They're still looking at you," he notes matter- of-factly.

I can't stand up anymore, I can't run anymore. No energy. I take my hands from my head, press my forehead tightly into my knees, and, still not opening my eyes, start scratching open a hole underneath myself with my hands. Sanctuary. Shelter. The sand is dry and keeps trickling back, but I'm tough, persistent.

When I feel like I've dug down deep enough, I put my hands in front of my face, open my eyes, and peer through my fingers. Everything has changed. The sky is filled with clouds. The horizon is completely black over the sea. The wind is fling- ing about the hair of the many-headed throng and whipping around the towels, which they are hurriedly gathering up off the ground and shoving—sloppily folded—into brightly-colored beach totes and wrinkled supermarket bags. But they still don't take their eyes off me—even as they hurry away, to the last second, until they disappear over the dunes.

He has vanished too.

The wind rips the dry sand up into the air and twists it into vortices across the beach, it gradually covers the hollows made by reclining bodies, the depressions from heads and hips with its sandy scrawl.

"Get up. Let's go home."

Someone has come up quietly behind me and sticks their hands underneath my arms.

"Get up . . ." Valts says calmly as he lifts me up.

I let him. My legs are completely limp, I support myself against Valts's shoulder. I stop looking around, I don't want to see anyone, anything—no people, no eyes, no beach. Valts takes me home. We're quiet the whole way. Sand grains irritate the skin between my toes. Also the corners of my eyes, but I can't rub them clean because of the sand clinging to my hands, I wipe them on my dress, but can't get them completely clean.

"Did he come back again?" Valts asks when—embracing each other tightly—we finally go inside the house.

The open window is still swinging back and forth like the wing of a bird wounded by a hunter's rifle. I'm disgustingly dirty, sweaty, and sandy. I want to take a shower.

"Yes," I answer curtly, kick my slippers off, and go wash up.

I need to hurry, he's never come when Valts is nearby. I don't want him around while I'm washing. I don't want him around at all. . .

When I get out of the shower, wrapped in a big towel, a cascade of white summer rain is falling outside the window. Drops are smacking loudly into the windowpane and battering the delicate jasmine blossoms outside. I close the window, the rattle of the rain against the windowsill transforms into a continuous hiss.

"At the end of the week, we'll go visit Ingrīda. Together," Valts says. "Don't give the jewelry to Arons if he shows up. But I need to go out for a bit right now. Can I leave you alone? I'll be back in about a half hour."

"Alone. Yes, you can leave me alone . . ." I answer absentmindedly.

The hammers start pounding inside my head again. Maybe they never stopped, and I just didn't notice?

I look out the window as Valts runs with shoulders hunched through the rain to the gate. He looks like a middle-aged man trying to prove—to someone, maybe himself—that he's still young. I bet he thinks his gait is light and agile . . .

"He could've taken an umbrella," I think and then go get dressed.

The coolness and damp brought by the rain has crept into the house. I put on red linen pants and a snug, soft-knit white sweater. And cotton socks. My skin likes all of it. It feels nice and cozy.

My head aches a bit, but at least it's clear, so I get back to work. A project outline. Expenses. Co-financing. I'm managing, it's working out. Outside it keeps raining and raining . . .

I hear chirping from the jasmine bush, I can't distinguish birds by their appearance, let alone their voices, I just understand that it's not a seagull or a crow. I go to the window, but don't see who was chirping, even though it's gotten brighter, there is still an occasional raindrop, but it's not a steady murmuring rumble anymore, and the wind has settled down too. I unlatch the window, the aroma of jasmine is even more intense, fresher, I inhale deeply, deeply, filling every inch of my lungs with its scent.

Got to work. Got to work, no time tomorrow, and at the end of the week we're going to Riga, there's not much time. I sink back into the project again. The work is going well. But somewhere deep down in my awareness my earlier need to escape is poking at me in an indescribable way. Fear mixed with thrilling shivers of hope. Belief in the possibility of escape.

There's a knocking somewhere, those are branches again, knocking against walls, windowsills, window frames. Boards creek and I listen more carefully. Someone knocks quietly again and now I realize that there isn't any wind at all . . .

On the wooden steps by the doors of the veranda, leaning with her shoulder against the door jamb, there is a woman. A woman who isn't young anymore and quite clearly very tired.

"Good evening," she says.

I'm a little confused, but it must be after seven already. "Good evening?" I respond to her in an inquisitive tone.

"Do you know anyone who I could call to talk about this house?" She motions to a dilapidated building on the other side of our fence. "The phone number that's written on the sign is disconnected."

The hem of the woman's long, dark cotton skirt is wet and sandy, just like her bare feet in her soaking wet tourist sandals.

The armpits of her loose, gray T-shirt are sweaty under the shoulder straps of her giant backpack, and she has a bright yellow scarf around her head, wrapped like a turban. But she is soaked through and through, and she doesn't smell like she is homeless.

"I wanted to ask if I could spend the night there. One night, I've got a sleeping bag," she explains to me, even though I hadn't asked.

"The previous owner sold the house about five years ago. That number is from back then . . . But I don't know anything about the new owner, I don't think I'll be able to help you."

She stares at me for a moment, as if hoping I'd say something else. Then she sighs, tears her shoulder away from the door jamb, and trudges heavily down the three creaking wooden steps. When she is already halfway to the gate, I can't stop myself.

"Wait, maybe you'd like to have some tea or coffee?"

She stops and looks me in the eyes somewhat incredulously.

"Yes, yes, come in, maybe we'll also figure out where you can sleep tonight," I invite her in and that doesn't even surprise me . . . A moment later we're sitting at the large table in the front room, I've poured myself another black coffee, the stranger wanted green tea and I only had last year's peppermint in the pantry. Aromas of coffee and peppermint mix with jasmine and fill the room with a strange bouquet, which is vaguely reminiscent of incense at an occult ritual.

It's awkward, I don't really know how to keep a conversation going with a stranger, and she doesn't say anything either as she clutches the ample mug of tea with both hands. It must be hot, yet she doesn't pull her hands away.

"Are you traveling?"

She looks at me with surprise.

"No. Yes. I'm not traveling, I'm walking."

"Where to?".

She lets go of the mug, she presses her warm palms against her cheeks. Blue writing on the orange mug spells out the words "This is the best time of your life!" and a bumpy, black stripe stretches across it at an angle underlining the word "best."

"At first, I thought I knew . . . But now I've forgotten, so I'm just walking."

"For a long time?"

"Two winters have gone by. Don't ask me about it, please . . . I don't want to seem rude, but . . . I don't want to talk about it."

She clasps the mug with both hands again and raises it to her lips. I finally look carefully at her face and am startled. I feel like I've seen her somewhere. More tanned, more disheveled, older, more wrinkles around her eyes, and the corners of her lips deeper set, sharper than I remember. Maybe I'm wrong, sometimes complete strangers who have never met and who have no connection between them can look like twins. Astrological twins—the term suddenly pops into my mind from some childhood book. I decide not to delve too deeply within myself, searching for what this face reminds me of.

"I'm sorry. I probably sound ungrateful," she puts the mug down on the table again and lowers her eyes.

"No, it's fine," I answer calmly. "I'd of course like to know who I've let into my house. But it was my choice—to invite you in for tea."

And then I remember that when I'd invited her in, I'd mentioned a place to sleep tonight. Maybe it's only because this woman is here, maybe it's because she's hoping to find a roof under which to spend the night, that we're sitting together and struggling through this conversation of half words and half sentences. I start to open my mouth to say she can spend the night in the attic room, and that she can definitely use the shower, and that in a minute my husband will be home and I'll make dinner. Then I come to my senses and remember how Valts was already angry at me for trusting strangers and I understand that I can't make this decision on my own. When he left, he said he'd back in a half hour, I glance at the big clock on the wall—it's been hours now.

"You can call me Alise," she says quietly.

"Thank you, Alise. You won't mind if I go into the other room for a second? Make yourself at home." In my confusion I neglect to mention my name.

I walk through to the other room, to the end of the hallway, and end up in the unfinished room. I close the door tightly. Nobody will hear me here for certain. The phone rings for a long time, and out of habit I count. After the ninth ring, Valts finally picks up.

"No, no, no!" Valts angrily and anxiously snaps back after listening to my hurried story. "No, what's wrong with you? Where is she now, you left her by herself? In our house?"

"Listen, I . . ."

"No. If you absolutely won't throw her out, then call a few hotels. If it's not too expensive, I'll pay for it."

He hangs up before I can ask him where he is and why he hasn't come home. In the background I hear a quiet din, all too familiar to me . . .

I go back to the stranger, she's sitting in the same stooped position as when I left her, except for her yellow turban, which she has taken off. Dark gray hair with silver locks, it's sweat-soaked in places where it appears completely black. I walk over to the computer and turn on the speakers, I click something on YouTube and the room fills with gentle, soothing piano music. I sit back down across from Alise.

"Debussy . . ." she says and her face stretches into a delighted expression. A moment later she adds: "The Arabesques."

I smile stupidly and don't answer. I have no idea what's playing, I don't know a thing about serious music, I like listening to it, especially the piano, when I'm working around the house, by myself, but usually I just click on a playlist on YouTube or Spotify and let it run without paying any attention to the names of the composers or the pieces . . . I want to get up and go look, but I somehow feel uncomfortable under Alise's probing gaze.

"It's hard to live with people who believe things like that, isn't it?" she asks suddenly. And looks closer at me. I don't understand what she means by that, and again it feels like I've seen her somewhere else before.

I look down and notice that my fingers are braiding the tassels on the tablecloth. Methodically, one after another, each group of three tassels has been braided into tight, neat, little braids, my hands now are braiding a fourth one. I finish braiding it, press it together with my hands so it stays together, and refrain from touching the next set of tassels. I should keep working, I should talk to her about hotels or at least offer her a shower, or start making dinner, it doesn't look like she's eaten all that well lately. But I sit, listen, and can't force a single logical sentence across my lips.

"I wanted to run away," she says. "But everything turned out to be such a mess. I couldn't understand what I was running from or where it even was . . . Outside or inside of me. But I'm on my way, and the way is open for me in every direction, I can go anywhere at any time, though I no longer understand which is the way back. No, honestly, I'm not even trying to find it. I don't know if I want to go back. And as long as I don't know, I keep going, not fully understanding where I'm really headed—further and further away or just in circles . . . But if someone were to ask me, now, what they should do if they wanted to run away, I'd say—stay. Don't run."

A twinge of pain shoots through my head again, she's answering the questions I'm afraid to ask. Questions about myself.

"Why are you telling me all of this, Alise?"

Alise lifts the mug of now mostly cool tea to her lips, but when she puts it down on the table and wants to say something else, my phone rings. It's Valts. I grab it and leave again, but this time just in the next room. I know that Alise won't hear the conversation, there's still piano music playing and again I've got no idea by whom or what. But it's playing.

"Valts, where are you, why aren't you home yet?" I ask without greeting him as I press the talk button. "You're at the casino, right? Don't lie, you're gambling again!"

"Is that woman still there with you?" Valts doesn't answer my question.

"Yes, she's drinking tea, I haven't said anything about a hotel. Valts, I'm afraid of her. She's kind of, I don't know, strange . . ."

"You're the one who let her in the house! Fine. Give her the phone, I'll talk to her."

"You don't need to, she's not doing anything bad. Come home, I want you to be home."

I'm listening as I talk. Valts isn't at the casino anymore. It feels like there are distant street noises in the background. Maybe earlier it was just my imagination? My fear?

"I'll be home soon. In about ten minutes."

Ten minutes feel like an eternity to me right now. I'll go and tell her that this is it, enough, I need to work. Thank God I didn't start talking to her about a place to spend the night, about the attic room or a hotel. She can leave, she can find her own path, byways, and way back, she can walk in circles and loops just as long as she disappears forever.

I walk resolutely into the front room and as I close the door, there are tough and direct words on the tip of my tongue: "Well, it's time for you to go."

But there's nobody sitting at the table anymore. I didn't hear her leave while I was talking to Valts. I walk out into the yard, rush over to the gate, lean over it, and look in both directions. There's nobody on the street either.

"Impossible," I think, my hand resting on the gate post lightly trembling.

When Valts comes in, I've already washed both mugs and am sitting on the old Vienna chair hugging my knees.

"Where is she?" Valts asks and I hear that he's annoyed.

"Gone. She left," I say and press my forehead into my knees.

"Why did you even let her in?"

"I invited her in for tea," I correct him without lifting my head.

Valts doesn't say anything. I hear him walking back and forth and I feel like any word that I'd say would flash like a bolt of lightning between us and come crashing down like thunder.

"You were at the casino, weren't you," I finally say as indifferently as I can and lift my gaze toward Valts. There's no crash. Valts turns around, walks out the door, slamming it behind him, and a few seconds later the gate creaks and slams shut too. Outside, twilight has nearly turned to darkness.

I don't get up from the chair. The air thickens and keeps getting darker, evening sounds flow in through the open window. People walk by on the other side of the fence, quietly talking to each other. Swooping overhead, seagulls cry out despairingly. Something rustles in the jasmine—maybe the neighbors' cat? And then the gate creaks again, and a moment later Valts comes into the room and turns on the light.

"Someday you'll leave and won't come back, right?" I ask.

My eyes, dazzled by the light, don't meet his gaze.

"Maybe. I don't know . . ." Valts answers quietly.

"How did you know I was at the beach? Earlier today."

"I got a call that you were running around again, and . . ."

"I didn't make dinner," I don't let him finish the sentence. I don't want to know who was reporting to Valts about his crazy wife this time. "Do you want some pelmeņi? It's late, I'm not going to manage anything else."

"Then pelmeņi it is."

I finally lower my feet to the floor, they tingle a bit and are a little wobbly as I walk to the kitchen. I pour water into a pot and put it on the gas stove, I add salt and some seasoning and wait for it to boil. I take the pelmeņi out of the freezer and give them a good shake, so that they aren't stuck together.

"How did you like her?" a familiar voice suddenly whispers in my ear, rustling my hair with its breath. I shudder, the box of pelmeņi slips from my hands and falls with a crash onto the floor.

"What happened in there?" Valts calls out from the other room.

I pick the box up off the floor.

"Nothing," I answer my husband.

The water boils and I carefully pour the frozen lumps of dough and meat into the piping hot liquid. There's a knife sitting next to me on the kitchen cabinet, Valts sharpened it yesterday like a razor. I'm looking at the glittering blade and know that one quick and easy slice would be the easiest exit from this nightmare, this powerlessness, this shifting between phantoms and reality. I put my fingers on my neck until I find where I can feel my pulse, maybe that's my carotid artery, I don't know, but certainly there, under my skin, there's blood flowing through this vessel.

"You won't. You're afraid, aren't you?" I feel like maybe finally I hear a tinge of fear in his whispering, his always arrogant tone has vanished, yes, he's terrified, his life will flow away together with my blood, his image will dissolve into oblivion along with me, there won't be anyone to remember, mention, or long for him. Because I'll be dead.

"You don't have the guts!" the hysterical whisper tries to sound derisive.

Without removing my fingers from the pulsing vessel under my skin, I reach for the knife.

"Are you crazy? What are you doing?"

Valts grabs my outstretched hand, yanks it away, and pulls it up to himself. The hand that was pressed against my neck twists awkwardly and stays between us. Valts is holding me frantically, desperately, and helplessly. But with all his strength.

"I wouldn't have done it," I say and hear how somewhere in the corner someone is laughing wildly, out of breath, choking, until they finally start to cough. And then silence.

Valts doesn't let me go, over his shoulder I see a magazine cover. An old, stained magazine cover that has been placed there only so that there is a spot to put a hot pot or pan when taking it off the stove. Gazing at me from the cover is the stranger from a moment ago in a light, airy blouse with stylishly contoured eyes, colored and styled hair, and a warm hint of a smile. Younger and completely different, but it's Alise. "Businesswoman Alise Reinholde: I finally feel loved and appreciated"—white letters announce across the lapel of her cherry-colored jacket.

"Can you hear me?" Valts asks in a tired voice, and I realize that while I was studying the old magazine over his shoulder, he had said something. I press my cheek against his shoulder. "I asked if that woman really was here?"

"I don't know, Valts."

I really don't know. Valts lets me go but doesn't take his eyes off of me. The pelmeņi have long ago overcooked, their flour casings have come apart into a thick bubbling goo. I turn off the gas. I don't feel like eating. Valts doesn't seem to either because he says:

"Let's go to bed. Tomorrow first thing let's go see Helmuts. Are you okay with that?"

Helmuts is my psychiatrist. We have been together for twelve years. My invisible guest has been visiting and talking to me since I was a teenager, but no matter how silly it sounds, until I started seeing Helmuts, I was convinced it was nothing special. That this is just how it is. That everyone has a friend they talk to when they're all alone . . . Who might sometimes suggest or even demand something, and sometimes even completely muddle your mind.

I'm tired and just nod, "Yeah, let's go."

"I should take a shower, but I'm afraid to leave you . . ."

"It'll be okay," I answer indifferently and wait until he gets in the shower, I wait until I can get to the old magazine and read about Alise. "I promise."

He doesn't believe me, I can tell, but he walks to the bathroom anyway.

When I hear the water hissing in the shower, I take the battered magazine and sit down right there in the kitchen on the low wooden bench that I usually use for peeling potatoes. The issue is three years and two months old. Unbelievable . . . She looked at least fifteen years older today . . . I open it and leaf through it looking for the article that I definitely have to read, the one where I can find the hints, nuances, and messages that intuition can interpret, and which will tell me what happens next. What happened next. I turn page after page until I find the photo spread. Alise with a man, her shoulder pressed confidently against his chest, but her chin resting lightly against his hair. Bright and warm gazes for the camera.

There's nothing else. Confused, I look at the next page where there is a photo of some kind of casserole and all the ingredients—in liters and lengths—needed for its preparation detailed next to it. I anxiously thumb back and forth through the magazine, my fingers don't listen, the pages are stuck together, but finally I noticed the page numbers, eight pages are missing after the large, bright photograph . . .

"I feel like I'm being kept in a cage," Valts says when I'm already in bed.

The sky is completely clear again and the round moon brightly illuminates the bedroom almost as if it were day. But everything is monochrome.

"You're going to leave," I whisper.

"I want out. I really want out. This isn't the life that I'd ever planned."

"I understand . . ."

"You don't understand shit . . ." he sighs. "It's a dead end. A trap. I can't leave you because you'll fall apart, and then I won't be able to live with myself. You need someone to take care of you and who else can do it better than me, I wouldn't trust anyone else. But by staying, I'm falling apart."

I've got no words. I'm lying next to him—without fear, without desperation, without the desire to keep him here. And without any dreams for the future. Not together. Not alone. Not with anybody else. Then it occurs to me that maybe an hour ago I did actually manage to slice through the tissues in my neck—skin, flesh, pulsing veins—and that everything that's happened since then is actually just the nightmares of my final agonies as I slowly bleed out . . .

We're quiet for a moment longer, then arrange ourselves to fall asleep. We turn our backs to each other and press together tightly. Our body heat and the peace it brings slowly flow between us, it embraces our bodies, and soon I hear Valts starting to snore quietly. My body also gradually relaxes, and I release myself calmly to sleep. I feel someone sit down at the foot of the bed, on my side. I can't tell—if there's one or two of them sitting there . . .

And then I fall asleep.

RUNAWAY TRAIN

Dāvids comes into the room. He sets his gym bag on the ground with a thud, almost as if it were full of rocks. Vanesa looks at her brother, unable to say a word, happiness and excitement practically taking her breath away.

"You're all grown up," she finally says and wraps him in a tight hug, rests her cheek against his shoulder and inhales deeply.

Vanesa breathes in the aroma of laundry detergent and warm skin, which mix with another smell that she doesn't like, but she ignores it, pushing away the unpleasant scent and inhaling again deeply.

"You're all grown up," she repeats, releasing him and looking deeply into Dāvids's face. "I haven't seen you in so long."

Dāvids smiles and looks over her. It's the same crooked smile from childhood. Vanesa tries to catch her little brother's gaze, but he's gotten a lot taller than his sister and she would need to take a few steps back to look into his eyes.

"Say something," Vanesa laughs and hugs her brother again, this time wrapping her arms around his strong, fit chest.

The unpleasant odor wafts up again and Vanesa, pressing her ear against Dāvids's chest, tries to hear her brother's heartbeat. But she can't hear anything. Vanesa holds her breath for a moment, but still hears nothing. She pushes the air out of her lungs quickly and then breathes in deeply, and now the smell of decay in the room is much stronger than any of the other smells. Dāvids stands firmly like a figure cut from wood, then moves suddenly, and Vanesa is so startled by the abrupt movement that she jumps to the side, tripping over the heavy bag and ripping it open with her foot as she falls.

It really is full of rocks. Dirty, wet, slimy rocks. Mixed with bones of varying size. And all of it smells of decay.

Vanesa looks up. Dāvids is gone.

When she wakes, Vanesa doesn't want to open her eyes for a long time. Dāvids had come to her in her dreams again, and once more she hadn't been able to keep her brother here. To hug him tightly enough to drag him out of her dream and into reality when waking up. Here. Next to her.

"How stupid," she mutters, awareness gradually sharpening.

It's Saturday morning and the alarm is off, but this time Vanesa can't afford to spend all day in bed, sleep mixing incoherently with moments of wakefulness, not showering, not eating, not caring about phone calls or the pings from Messenger.

Today is Dāvids's birthday. February sixteenth.

Her brother is turning twenty.

Today—like every year—Vanesa will drive out to the countryside to be with her parents. And just like every year, her parents' house—called "Rietumi"—is the place where she least wants to be on this day. Someday she'll run away from it all. But not yet, she's not ready yet. She still feels bad for her mom and her old man, to hell with them both. Mom called yesterday to tell her that her right shoulder and elbow hurt very much and that she probably won't be able to bake a cake.

"The farm's always coming apart at the seams, the owner doesn't give a crap that I don't have a winter coat, and he doesn't care about the calves either, if anything happens it'll be my fault, if anyone catches bronchitis, but it hurts like crazy, having to work in this freezing draft, so that I'm bent over from the pain, there's no way I can manage to mix everything together for a cake . . ." her voice gradually chokes with the tears she's been holding back. "Then don't bake it. Maybe we'll be fine this time without it?" Vanesa says as her mother's floodgates open.

Muttering, moaning, and sniffling, she sobs for a moment into the phone, trying to say something, until Vanesa can't take it anymore.

"I can buy one," she offers, "just this once we can eat a store-bought cake, can't we?"

Mom gradually calms down. "You'd do that?"

"Of course, why wouldn't I?"

Over the years, whenever Mom has baked a cake, they've never finished it. Everyone nibbles at their piece, trying to force down each bite. Vanesa has no idea where the remaining uneaten two thirds of it end up every time. She never spends the night at the house, but drives back to the city.

At the market, two bakery counters stand next to one another, both have all kinds of cakes—with meringue, with gelatin, chocolate, coffee, fruit, cream cheese. Vanesa's eyes gloss over staring at the selection. She gazes helplessly at the sweet peaks fringed with cream roses and marzipan trifles and can't make up her mind. As if it even mattered.

"Miss, can I help you?"

The seller is a gaunt, middle-aged woman with an upper lip that's too short and big, prominent front teeth. When she smiles, they seem to push forward and hang over her bottom lip.

"I need a cake," Vanesa says sorrowfully, as if standing in front of the display case for a few minutes and staring bewildered at the selection wouldn't have clearly testified to her need.

"What kind of cakes do you like—lighter, heavier, with fruit, with meringue, chocolate, caramel, cream, or whipped cream? This one is cream cheese with bits of pineapple, this one is made from sour cream, really tasty, there's strawberry jam between each layer, but this one, look, this one is really airy, just gently beaten egg whites with lightly cooked cream and fresh berries, this one gets bought a lot, but if you want one with real buttercream, then there's our "Chocolate Dream," the layers of sponge cake are soaked with a bit of rum, not rum extract, but with real rum, and . . ." Vanesa is unable to receive and comprehend what the clerk is saying, she just pulls money out of the wallet in her purse and points a finger at the display case.

"An excellent choice, would you like the small one or the big one?"

"The big one," Vanesa grunts. She doesn't care.

"That'll be seven euros and forty cents." The seller carefully ties string around the cake box, she's not smiling anymore, and it seems like she has to work to keep her short upper lip over her front teeth so that it doesn't spring up. Vanesa didn't notice which cake the seller wrapped up, but it really doesn't matter at all.

September 24, 2012

I've already gotten used to it. There's three of us sharing the room, but it doesn't bother me, I shared a room with my sister after all. Annija and Marta are both from Līvāni, from the same school, they stick together, they're nice to me, but keep their distance. Well, sure, they've known each other a long time, I'm a stranger. There's sixteen of us in my course, but I haven't made any friends yet. Only girls. That's funny because boys can also study to be and work as gardeners.

I'm getting my scholarship on October 3rd, a whole 50 lats! I've got almost no money. I should've worked for at least another week in the summer, I would've gotten another ten, but I couldn't, my parents were off the wagon again, and I had to go home. I had to cook for my siblings, put together their clothes for school, pack my own bags for college. And most importantly, make sure my old man didn't screw things up. Mom always blacks out pretty fast, and then he walks around picking fights. I don't know how they'll get on without me. Selīna doesn't get as much, she's smaller and knows how to hide, but Dāvids talks back. I told him he should just go over to a friend's place, like Salvis or Aleksis, if he sees the old man going nuts. Better go over to Salvis's, he's got normal parents, but if not, then Aleksis isn't far away either.

I haven't gone home yet, no reason to, but on the first Sunday of October after I get my scholarship, I'll be able to.

(Continued later in the evening)

Selīna just called and said our parents had been boozing again on Saturday and got into a fight. After beating up Mom, the old man went after Dāvids. Dāvids ran away and still hasn't come home. It's already Monday. Selīna said that he wasn't at school either and he's not answering his phone. I tried, and he really won't answer. I told her to run over to Salvis's house, if he's not there, then to Aleksis's. Why didn't I think to get their phone numbers? That's no good, skipping school, I'll come back home, give him a talking to. He still listens to me some, but he's a bit out of control.

I'd hoped that after the August parties our parents would hold it together for a while . . . Where do they get the money? They're probably in debt again. Unemployment pays next to nothing and it'll soon end for both of them anyway.

The large cake doesn't really seem all that large. Lifting it up it looks like it's maybe half the size of one of mom's cakes.

Vanesa puts the round box into the trunk of her car, wrapped in newspapers so that it doesn't freeze, there are a couple of cyclamens already there—a blood red one for mom and a white one for Selīna. She never did become a gardener, but her one-room apartment is still filled with plants, on every shelf, on the tables and cabinets, and during the summer all the windowsills are crammed full of pots of petunias, geraniums, lobelias, begonias, and Vanesa always brings something green and blooming to brighten up her mom's and sister's rooms. Selīna is usually happy about it, but Mom sighs.

Vanesa gets in the car. It's cold, so she doesn't want to take off her gloves. She starts the engine, turns on the heater, and clicks on the radio. And just as quickly clicks it off again. It's that song. Just one bar, not even a melody yet, or even a word, just two rock guitar chords. Vanesa knows them. It's that song. Today she doesn't need that at all.

Five minutes later the inside of the car is warm and Vanesa turns the radio back on, and just in case she tunes it to a different station, because songs usually get played on a loop, repeating after a certain amount of time in the same order. Then she drives out onto the street. It's an hour and a half trip. The moments she has behind the wheel are the calmest in the otherwise abnormal rhythm of Vanesa's life. You sit there calmly, just driving. And thinking. It's not easy. It's easier to race morning to night to wherever the boss says, to get letters, applications, to look for information, check emails, write responses, make and bring coffee that's just the right strength—one kind of right strength for the morning, another for the afternoon. To prepare documents, join the boss in meetings, order office supplies, and it all keeps going, going, going. In the evening after the gym, take a shower, turn on whatever show, and, snacking on apple, fall asleep twenty minutes later . . .

Vanesa drives and thinks about Selīna. Of the three of them, her sister is the most insecure, the most timid. She's been like that since childhood. She does well in school and reads a lot. But what does any of that matter if she never leaves the house.

Despite her mediocre accomplishments, Vanesa has been completely independent financially from her parents since she was sixteen. She always found some little job, some farmer who needed help during the summer, or a summer camp at the elementary school during other summers where she worked in the kitchen, peeled potatoes, washed dishes, cleaned up the mess hall. Fast and clever, she managed to do everything quickly and carefully. It wasn't hard. Just those early mornings, but you can do anything for a month. And in the winter—during school—she found elsewhere to make money. Agnese lived with her two kids in a house across the road toward the center of town while her husband was in Ireland. Every other week she worked the night shift at the fish cannery, and after school Vanesa would watch her kids, Kristiana and Nellija, twins in first grade. Sometimes also on weekends when Agnese wanted a little bit more freedom and fun. Her mom would always sneer when she was drunk, "The village bicycle, I guess her wheels are itching again." But that wasn't Vanesa's business, Agnese always paid her for taking care of the kids, as agreed. Plus, it was usually quieter at Agnese's house than at "Rietumi."

Selīna is eighteen, but she only leaves the house in the morning to walk to the school bus, and straight back again in the evening. Pale, gangly, she probably doesn't have any girl-friends either. Vanesa sometimes brings her a more stylish skirt, jacket, or high heels. When she has her try them on, her sister obliges, twirls in front of the mirror, seems happy, but when Vanesa comes back home, all of it is sitting on the nice clothes shelf, just like when she left. It looks to Vanesa like they haven't moved since she'd folded and put them away.

"Where would I even wear those clothes?" Selīna says, hearing her sister sigh at the open closet door.

She's all talk, but never looks away from her phone or laptop. Vanesa wants to know what she's looking at, what matters to her, there are just black-and-white videos or long texts in

English flashing on her screen, but when Selīna notices her sister's curiosity, she always just angrily shuts her phone or laptop so that Vanesa can't see.

Maybe something will change after high school. She'll go to college, she'll definitely get funding, but the main thing—she'll be out of that house. It seems to Vanesa that the ground, the walls, the air, and people's hearts here are soaked with black bile . . . When you're there you can't really see it, but when Vanesa thinks about her childhood home, all of her memories are suspended in a thick, black fog.

September 28, 2012

There was no time to write. I'm at home. It's already evening. Dāvids still hasn't come back. When he shows up, I'll give him a piece of my mind. I'll really give it to him. You just can't act like that. If you run away, you at least have to tell somebody close to you. It's fine if you don't want to say where you're going, but at least say that you left, and that it was by your own choice. Otherwise, all kinds of terrible thoughts fill your head. Selīna is pure panic, I'm trying to calm her down, Dāvids isn't a little boy, after all, he's thirteen, and he's got a head on his shoulders. His anger and hurt will pass, and then he'll come home, where else can he go. But I can't calm Selīna down. On the phone she can't catch her breath between sobs, what else could I do? So I came home. I tried to borrow money from Annija and Marta, but they said that money was really tight until the scholarship comes in. I stole a ride on the train and hitchhiked. It worked out, I didn't have to wait for long, a man in a white car took me all the way to the town center. I'd never met someone like that, he didn't say much at all, just asked where I needed to go. I also didn't try to talk. He kept drinking Coke out of a glass bottle the whole time. Gulping it down with this weird glug in his throat, I'd never heard anything like that, somebody gulping down a drink so loudly, I could even hear it over the engine.

Mom was starting to come around. She asked where Dāvids was. I told her that I should be asking her that. Selīna started crying again, yelling at Mom, "I've been telling you every day that Dāvids went somewhere and isn't back, what's wrong with you, don't you understand?" Mom didn't say anything, but I could see she was twisted up in knots, who knows if she even really understands anything, she still has to get through today somehow, then tomorrow she'll start being able to talk normally. The old man is still passed out.

Selīna told her what happened that day. The old man had made Mom go to the store and get a fifth on credit, but Mom said that on Saturday they were open only until two and it was already two-thirty, but you can't convince the old man of anything. He started shaking Mom, pulling her hair, and Dāvids got in the middle. He started kicking the old man, who stopped beating Mom and started going after Dāvids. He staggered around and couldn't catch him, then started to swear at him. Dāvids just laughed until the old man screamed, "You better not show your crooked face around here again, if I find you, I'll tear you to pieces." Dāvids ran into the bushes behind the shed and when the old man stumbled around the back of the house, probably to piss all over the kitchen windowsill again, Dāvids ran inside, grabbed his school bag, stuffed some things in it, and ran off. Selīna asked him where he was going, but he didn't say anything.

Okay. I'll talk to Mom tomorrow. Saturday or Sunday we have to get Dāvids home, so I can go back to school.

Vanesa turns off of the wide, smooth highway. It's fifty more kilometers until her destination, and now she has to drive more slowly and carefully, around here, some parts of the asphalt are nothing but potholes, and every now and again there are still unsalted patches of ice from the last snow—melted, driven over, and frozen again.

Her cell phone rings. Vanesa turns down the radio and flips open her phone. It's Rihards. Rihards on a Saturday! That means she needs to pull over. Other times Vanesa talks while driving, but this time she pulls the car over on the side of the road and answers.

"Yes, Rihards!"

"Hey! What are you up to? We can meet right now, I've suddenly got three hours free."

Vanesa is tapping her knee with the fingers of her left hand. "I can't . . . I'm driving to my parents' place."

"How far are you? Turn around and come back!"

Rihards laughs, but Vanesa can already hear a tinge of annoyance in his laughter.

"It's my brother's birthday today. I have to go."

"Your brother? You've got a brother? Since when? Why am I only finding out about him now?"

"I can't tell you everything right from the start, I have to leave a few surprises," Vanesa tries to joke, but knows it sounds totally clumsy.

"What's his name? How old is he going to be?"

Rihards is upset, and Vanesa feels a bit guilty that she didn't tell him earlier, but she doesn't usually tell just anybody about Dāvids right away. Rihards isn't "just anybody," of course, but Vanesa also doesn't really know what exactly he is to her.

Her boyfriend.

Her married boyfriend.

"Dāvids is turning twenty today," she answers obligingly.

"So, you're having a big fucking bash?"

Rihards isn't trying to hide his annoyed tone with laughter anymore.

"No," Vanesa answers curtly.

"With your brother's friends and other players," Rihards doesn't quit. Vanesa doesn't even try answering. It's the wrong time to tell him about Dāvids. There's no one there to hear or listen.

"Okay! Have fun!" Rihards yells and the call cuts off.

Vanesa shuts her phone and puts it away, and stares straight ahead for a moment. A short ways ahead, maybe sixty meters from her, a fox saunters out of the forest, with a thick, dense coat, that—from a distance—looks like it's covered in frost. It walks out to the edge of the road, then stops and, bending its black legs gently at the knees, ready to leap in an instant, carefully studies the red Fiat parked on the shoulder. Vanesa is sure that the fox is staring right into her eyes through the windshield, so she doesn't blink at all. She shuts off the engine. The fox is still in the same pose and looks as if it were stuffed, it seems to Vanesa that the animal's eyes are gently flickering with a red glow and that there's a recognizable, crooked, and mischievous smirk stretched across its muzzle. There's no wind, but even through the closed doors she can hear the pines creaking on both sides of the road. Then a car appears from around a distant curve, visible at first and audible only a moment later. The fox turns and calmly walks across the road, it stops for a moment, but doesn't look at Vanesa anymore, then jumps across the ditch, and disappears at a steady trot between the newly sprouted young spruces.

The white car zooms by and Vanesa starts up her car to continue on her way. If she hadn't exchanged glances with the fox, she might be feeling really awful.

October 2, 2012

I'm back at school, it's Tuesday, I didn't get back until now.

Yesterday Mom and I went to the police to submit a report. Dāvids hasn't been at Aleksis's or Salvis's. He hasn't been there at all, not even on Saturday. Nobody has seen him since he left the house. I'm afraid to even think about it, I don't know what to think. He must have gone somewhere if he packed his bag. He'd packed some clothes. Selīna said that he'd also grabbed a cucumber and a hunk of bread from the kitchen. Everybody knows him around here, so it can't be that nobody saw him anywhere. In the bright light of day.

The policeman we spoke to was really unfriendly. Mom didn't know what Dāvids was wearing, she called Selīna and then got confused, I wanted to tell her to stop, that I'll explain everything, but I couldn't get up the courage. I wasn't home that Saturday either. But does it matter that she was? I feel sorry for Mom, her hands were shaking, I could see that she was trying to hide them in her purse, but it was uncomfortable and awkward, the purse kept tipping forward, and as she spoke, she tried to grip it with her trembling hands. It seemed like no matter what the policeman was trying to get Mom to say, it wasn't true. Whatever else he might've done, he'd never left home without telling somebody. If he spent the night at a friend's house, Mom or Selīna always knew about it.

"No, he never just wanders around by himself," Mom said, and it looked to me that the policeman was getting even more annoyed, he just asked why we'd waited so long to submit a report.

Mom didn't say anything . . . We also couldn't find any good photographs. There was one where he was ten, but he's older now. A few online from Draugiem.lv, but in all of them he isn't facing the camera, maybe he just felt self-consciousness about his messy appearance, and I don't think anybody would recognize him from those pictures anyway.

In the end the police officer said that tomorrow, that is, today, he'd drive over to the house with a social worker and something else, I don't remember. But I had to be there. I told Mom just not to start drinking again. She answered, "Never again in my life." I don't believe her. When Dāvids shows up, she'll be so happy she'll get drunk again right away . . .

Today there's a report everywhere on the internet that he's missing. They'd used that picture of Dāvids when he was ten and also one from a social media profile. It's good that we each have our own last name, nobody here knows that he's my brother.

Vanesa drives the Fiat into the yard by "Rietumi" and backs into her usual spot next to the woodshed. The wind's moans drive a scattering of snow across the shrub-covered field, but above the distant woods a giant heap of pigeon-gray clouds is rising and approaching at a nearly imperceptible pace. Every so often, a white light flashes within it, but there's no thunder. The front door opens and through it tumbles her mother all bundled up, Selīna, and a giant, gray ball of fluff—Gorodvojs. When Dāvids left, Gorodvojs, her brother's favorite and the apple of his eye, was still living on a chain, and nobody had the idea back then to let him loose so he could help in the search. Vanesa didn't think of it either, but she only arrived a week after Dāvids had disappeared . . . And during that time, it rained for two days straight . . . Nobody thought that Dāvids wouldn't come home. They thought he'd be back in three days, a week, six months.

Mom stays in the doorway, but Selīna and Gorodvojs come to greet her out in the yard. Vanesa hugs her sister and then leans down to ruffle the dog's bushy coat. Gorodvojs licks his lips contentedly.

Vanesa takes the cake, the cyclamens, and a bag of snacks from the trunk, she hands some of it to her sister and takes some herself, and then they walk toward the house. The swollen sky is much closer now, and the wind's moans have grown more frequent and baleful. Mom smiles, strokes Vanesa's shoulder, and holds the door open so everyone can get inside. Gorodvojs too.

The old man is sitting at the kitchen table, his eyes completely glossy. Vanesa would be surprised if it were any other way.

"Hi!" she says, pulling out a half liter bottle of liquor and sets it down on the table.

The old man can't hide his joy, he coughs and rubs his palms against his filthy pants flecked with grease stains, but doesn't dare unscrew the top and pour the fiery liquid straight out of the bottle and down into his desiccated innards, right there on the spot, without waiting.

Sometimes Vanesa wonders how Mom met the old man. What about him did she come to like, why did she want to marry him, have his children, live together with him day to day, year to year, eat at the same table, sleep in the same bed? Beautiful, crazy Astrīda, with her black, curly hair, brown, stubborn eyes, a mouth like a stockyard gate, nobody could keep her from speaking her mind. And Gints—just as wild. Like flame against flame. Vanesa doesn't remember a time when Gints wasn't there, he turned up at "Rietumi" when she was a year-and-a-half old. A few months later, Astrīda's mother—a woman equally beautiful and strong, in her best years—was suddenly taken from them, in a week's time, by a stroke.

In their wedding photo, Gints is still good-looking, but already with features slightly disfigured and a gaze clouded over by liquor. Two-year-old Dāvids is sitting on Gints's knee, embraced by his father's strong hands, and Mom, smiling with bright red lips, pressed against her new husband's shoulder. Her dark eyes flickering. One imagines from joy . . . Vanesa, dressed up in a light-blue princess skirt, looking sullen, standing between the two of them. Who can even remember what wasn't to her liking again back then. Vanesa was only five years old. And Mom had a big stomach. Selīna was born two weeks after the wedding.

Vanesa knows who her father is. She's always known that it wasn't Gints, but he never treated Vanesa any better or worse than his own kids. But honestly, maybe in some ways better, because he never hit her. Selīna either though. But he would pummel Mom when he was drunk without it weighing on his conscience at all.

When did she start drinking with the old man? And why? Vanesa doesn't know . . . But she remembers the day well when Mom, drunk after her daily beating, had crawled into the shed or up into the attic somewhere to sleep and the old man had screamed and gone nuts in the yard, shaking his fists. Vanesa covered her ears with her hands and tried to read a book in the sisters' room, but through her palms she could still hear Selīna screaming:

"Mooommmmm, Mommy, Mooommmyyy!"

She threw down her book and ran outside into the yard at just the moment when the old man had drawn his heavy fist far back and hurtled it into Dāvids's already-blood-soaked face. Vanesa had never been afraid of the old man. She picked up the first log she could find and slammed it into his back. Teetering around his axis, he stared for a moment with red, bulging eyes at Vanesa. Selīna kept screaming.

The old man slunk off. Dāvids's eyebrow was split, he was crying, and the blood covering his face mixed with his tears and saliva and dripped onto his blue-striped polo shirt. There was no use trying to wake up Mom . . . Vanesa dressed his wound as best as she could. But it healed well, without a scar. And it was only about a week later that Vanesa noticed that the second, apparently heavier punch had rendered the left side of his face stiff, immobile. Dāvids had been only eight years old back then.

But Vanesa's father, Arvils, was living a quiet life with his wife and two children of about the same age as Dāvids and Selīna, he

141

worked as a bus driver, on weekdays he'd transport schoolchildren, but on weekends—residents from their township to Riga, to the theater and concerts, and Vanesa felt like he doesn't even remember that she is his child. Well, right, on Vanesa's birth certificate, there's a blank spot where her father's name should be. She'd never caught Arvils's glance, never noticed any awkwardness or a different attitude from him. Vanesa was one of many schoolchildren that he would transport. Except she had the same thin arched eyebrows as Arvils and the same rather large gap between her front teeth. Vanesa doesn't have that anymore. Those were her first big expenses she allowed herself when she started earning enough money to set some aside.

October 8, 2012

I'm back at "Rietumi" again. I'll probably stay here. I'll just drive to the nearby school and back home every night. I can't live anywhere else, everything is going to hell here. I can still study to be a gardener after I'm done with school.

Dāvids still isn't back. I don't know if I feel more scared or angry. But I still don't really believe that anything bad happened to him. I think he was tired of all of the abuse, and he just wanted to get away. Maybe he's built a lean-to out of tree branches somewhere in the forest, is angry and not coming home. We have to wait a few more weeks until it gets below freezing. He doesn't have money. There's no way he could. What's he eating? What's he covering himself with, what's he wearing? It's not the sunny side of September anymore, nights are only getting colder.

The police drove around the township asking residents if they'd seen Dāvids on the Saturday or Sunday when he'd left. Or if they'd seen anything suspicious at all on those days. Some of them re-membered seeing a white car driving around for several days with a strange man behind the wheel. But they couldn't remember if it was on those exact days. Maybe it was the same man who took me from the highway to the center. But that was after Dāvids disap-peared. Who this person was, nobody knows.

Mom and the old man have turned totally gray and weak, their cheeks are sunken, and the skin around their eyes has gotten even more wrinkled. They look like they're sixty, but Mom isn't even forty yet . . . The old man is still drinking, but he doesn't curse any-more or lay a hand on anyone, he walks around the house hunched over, looking like he doesn't know what to do with himself. He doesn't go outside much. Mom truly isn't drinking a drop right now. Every day we walk around the surrounding area. Ditches, bushes, the woods, the fields, Mom is always calling for Dāvids. Sometimes I think that she shouldn't, if he's hiding then he'll just go deeper and won't answer. But I don't tell Mom to stop. Sometimes someone who has some free time just then will come with us, Salvis and Aleksis with their parents, the men from the sawmill, and even its owner, this week some forty volunteers came here from the city. We walked through the underbrush, forming a chain, and then through the forest.

I can't sleep at night.

Vanesa takes her purchases out of the bag and puts them on the table. Selīna unwraps them, cuts, rinses, and puts food into dishes. Mom doesn't help, just sits and watches as her daughters busy themselves, absentmindedly rubbing her aching shoulder, though she had already prepared the serving platters, cut up some of her own pickled cucumbers and mushrooms. When Vanesa lived here, there was never anything like that. Mom also didn't bake cakes back then.

Vanesa gets a message on WhatsApp. It's Rihards.

"Sorry I got stressed, I thought we'd get to hang out. I'll call you tonight. What time is okay?"

Vanesa shuts off the wi-fi and sticks the phone in her purse.

Nobody talks, just white wisps behind the window whipping by ever faster. The gray cloud has covered the entire sky, and the snow strikes the window hard every so often. Mom is staring out the window right into the blizzard . . . Her gaze is ravenous, harrowed, and helpless. Her left palm keeps moving across her right shoulder and elbow, sliding up, down, up, down.

Vanesa wants to scream "He's not coming!" but swallows her rage.

She feels her anger—a black, stringy mass seething in her throat—she can't swallow it or spit it out. This is the last time. She's not coming back here to be with Mom and the old man on Dāvids's birthday again, there are three hundred sixty-four other days every year that she can visit them, no, three hundred sixty-three, the third Saturday in September is an even worse choice. Just today, just these three, four hours, watching Mom and the old man's silent self-flagellation, and she'll get in her red Fiat and drive home, drive back to her life filled with everything else, everything that has nothing to do with this world in which she grew up, with its stench of liquor and hangovers, its fights, swearing, poverty, and a desperate, unfulfilled longing to break free of this dank dump and forget about it forever.

Maybe, just maybe that would've happened too if Dāvids had come back . . . If he'd never left.

Mom doesn't even talk to the old man anymore. No, it's not out of hatred. Not even disgust or anger. They just don't have anything to talk about. Vanesa suspects that they never really did, but it's just that in their initial passion and then later on in their practically constant intoxicated state, Mom didn't notice. Since Dāvids's disappearance, she hasn't had a glass, a sip, a drop.

"How's life in the city?" suddenly coming to, Mom asks Vanesa.

"Good," Vanesa answers calmly, "I'm working, there's lots of work, not much free time."

"Do you have a boyfriend?"

"I don't have time for boyfriends, I just said that I've got lots of work."

Selīna has brought all of the dishes into Dāvids's room. Vanesa moves the cake from the box onto the large round tray, it turned out to be elegant, with chocolate cream and gelatin decorations, but looks absurdly small, the ones mom bakes usually cover the whole tray. Mom looks on and sighs, and again Vanesa has to stop herself from yelling:

"There's nothing to sigh about, who needs cake? You? The old man?"

But it's not just the cake that doesn't matter, saying any of that doesn't matter either. Vanesa grabs the tray with both hands and finally walks down to Dāvids's room.

The air in the room is stale, it smells of mold and old rags. Nothing has changed here for seven years. Just the first weekend after her last bender, Mom had cleaned the room, dusted it, organized Dāvids's clothes, picked up the dirty ones and washed them, carefully folding them afterward, putting them away in the old, narrow shelves of his closet. She put clean sheets on his bed. Even now, she still regularly does that, even though nobody sleeps there, Vanesa doesn't know how often she changes the sheets. Seventh-grade geography and English workbooks are sitting on the corner of the desk. Brand new, the only thing written on them is his name. Dāvids's photograph is sitting in a frame next to them, the one where he's ten years old. Mom had put it there later, Vanesa doesn't remember when exactly. There's a skateboard under the table, which Dāvids, blushing with joy, had brought home from Aleksis's a month before his disappearance when Aleksis's father had bought him a newer, cooler one. It was impossible to skate on the roads around here anyway, you had to go to the town center, to the paved roads and the running track by the elementary school. Aleksis didn't give Dāvids the board, just lent it to him so he could try it out, but when Dāvids left and never returned, Aleksis couldn't bring himself to take it back. Vanesa ran into him several times, and then she'd remind him to come get it, but Aleksis never came to their house again. Salvis didn't either, even though those first years Mom would always invite them both over for cake on Dāvids's birthday . . .

Nobody is allowed to put anything on Dāvids's desk. The old man has dragged in the little table from the TV room and now all the offerings were placed on top of it. The red cyclamen Vanesa brought is sitting on the windowsill. Pretty. Mom and Selīna are sitting on Dāvids's bed, two stools have been brought in from the kitchen, but the old man isn't there yet. Vanesa is standing. Her anger is still stuck in her throat, and she doesn't know whether to swallow it or spit it out. She stares out the window and the yard looks increasingly twilit, and the blizzard isn't letting up at all, it's only getting stronger, and every once in a while it flings another swirling fistful of snow.

Across the yard, lifting its black legs high out of the snow, a fox is trotting. It stops right in front of the window, it's sniffing something, sticks its nose in the snow, steps back, scratches at it with its forepaws, sniffs again, and finally lifts its head, looks in through the window and, catching sight of Vanesa, freezes. Through the blizzard she can't see if its eyes are flickering with fire, but strangely Vanesa doesn't even doubt that it's the same fox she saw earlier today crossing the road . . .

"Oh, the chips and Coke are still on the shelf."

Mom lurches up from the bed and totters down to the kitchen in her too-large slippers.

"It's a miracle that she's not in an evening dress and high heels," Vanesa thinks angrily, but she knows that Mom doesn't even have anything like that, and that's a good thing . . .

But she does have chips and Coke—the holiday treats that Dāvids always wanted but rarely got.

The table was set now. Piled high with goodies. Dāvids never experienced a party like this. Gorodvojs is sleeping on the ground, his shaggy body pressed against Selīna's leg and her black jeans. The old man has also finally showed up. A stench of liquor rises from him, it's clear that the half-liter Vanesa brought is already empty, but to take it along to Dāvids's room would be a shameless affront. They quietly place snacks, cheese

147

sandwiches, pickles, a handful of chips, and discs of smoked sausage onto their plates. Then, everyone takes their place and picks at their plates a little at a time . . . The old man is the only one with his mouth full, pickles and chips crunching sharply between his blackened teeth.

November 25, 2012

Dāvids isn't back. No one has found him. He hasn't come home. It looks like the police have no idea what happened to him. A few weeks ago, I had to go to the police and tell them about the man in the white car, whose portrait was immediately drawn based on my description. It turned out that the car had been driving around the country roads for several days and nobody knew who he was or what he was doing. Others had noticed that the car was a BMW, but I was the only who saw the driver up close. If only I'd known that I would need to remember the details of his face . . . I felt like the likeness that the artist drew was very similar. But I didn't know his eye color, I couldn't remember any distinguishing marks. They asked me if he was wearing a wedding ring or if he maybe had any tattoos on his hands, or anything else that stood out. There was nothing. Or I didn't see it. Just the nervous way he gulped that Coke. But even so, I don't believe he was involved. If that person had done anything to Dāvids, why would he have come back a few days later. It didn't make sense.

The head of the family court asked to meet with Mom and the old man. She came to see what our home life was like. She threatened to take Selīna and me out of the house too. When the police and social services came to the house for the first time after Dāvids's disappearance, Mom had been honest and said that she'd filed a report so late because she'd been on a bender and had been out of it. For now, Mom is holding on. But I understand that as soon as she gets into trouble, Selīna and I might end up at the orphanage.

The old man is drinking. I don't get it, does nothing matter to him? Dāvids was his only son. He keeps drinking, but doesn't lay a hand on anybody anymore . . .

I had a feeling that he knew something and was carefully and systematically trying to drink away his mind, his thoughts, maybe—his guilt? Maybe Dāvids came home that day or the next and the old man made good on his threats to tear him to pieces? Maybe he did it too well? I've carefully watched the old man's every step, every movement, I've tried to catch his gaze and stare closely and deeply at him—through all the liquor clouds and drunken whogivesashit. It seemed like he knew I was watching, because he started lurking around the shed and cellar.

It's hard. I still can't sleep through the night, If Dāvids is never found, I don't even know if that'll ever stop. I can't concentrate on my classes, but somehow I just keep pushing myself forward. I'm surprised about Selīna, she's doing well, better than ever. But she also doesn't do anything else. She reads, studies, digs around online. She seems obsessed.

Outside the window, the earth and sky are one. Snow is no longer being flung at the window, but the whistling and howling is constant, the blizzard keeps striking the pane and its swirling eddies make it impossible to see through it.

"I should go home," thinks Vanesa, "driving through this weather in the dark would be really dangerous."

Mom is already cutting the cake. It turns out that there's a mass of meringue baked into the middle layer, everything is crumbling and falling apart. Mom's injured arm is shaking, and crumbs of meringue are hitting the ground. Gorodvojs hops nimbly to his feet and collects each and every piece—no matter how tiny—with his big, wet tongue. Then, he sticks his hind end in the air, stretches his giant forepaws, sniffs every single nook and cranny around the floor, and with a lazy moan lets out a giant yawn, and returns to Selīna. He drops flat onto his stomach and rests his tired head on his paws.

Now everyone is poking around the crumbling remnants of the cake. Mom pours herself a glass of Coke and drinks loudly, gulping it down. Vanesa can't stand it anymore. She'd never heard her mother doing that. How can you even do that, how can you drink liquid with such loud, disgusting gulps!

Vanesa puts her unfinished plate of cake down on the table, it ends up being a little louder than she would've liked, and, without explaining, walks to Selīna's room. To the room that once had been hers. She walks in, plops onto her stomach on Selīna's bed, and decides to relax for three minutes and then go home. Not fall asleep, just relax.

Selīna comes in, it seems like she didn't get through all of her cake either, not that fast at least. Well, like always, like every year. She sits down on the bed next to her sister, and Vanesa hears her clicking around on her computer.

"Listen," Selīna says.

Vanesa thinks that her sister will keep talking, but she must have put on music, something is quietly crackling and buzzing, and then she connects the speakers, and with a heavy bass rhythm and a despairing guitar wail, a song bursts into the room.

"And watch this too, please, watch this."

Call you up in the middle of the night . . . Vanesa doesn't have to watch, she knows this clip by heart, every frame, every person, every street and building. Every child's name in the list and the year they disappeared. *So tired that I couldn't even sleep* . . . She doesn't want to listen, she can't, every chord, every word that he sings, and even the tone of this voice is one never-ending dead end, nothing will ever change.

Hope and faith have crumbled, fallen to pieces like the cake's meringue layer, scattered every which way never to be put together again. Runaway train never comin' back, wrong way on a one way track . . . He sings and sings, and doesn't stop, and the whole time Selīna tries to convince Vanesa to watch the clip.

Finally.

Finally the song is over.

Silence.

"You didn't watch it . . . It's Soul Asylum," Selīna says disappointedly. "A band."

"I know," Vanesa answers.

"They've put together pictures of kids and teens in the clip, who've disappeared without a trace in America in the nineties, their photo and the year they went missing, do you understand, Vanesa, thanks to the clip, twenty-one out of thirty-five have been found, some of the photographs have been switched out for others. Can you believe it? Do you understand?" Selīna's voice fills with the tears she's been holding back.

"I know," Vanesa says even more quietly.

"You knew about it and didn't tell me?"

"And how would it have helped? You wanted to send them Dāvids's photo?"

Vanesa finally turns toward her sister. Selīna is sitting with the computer open on her lap, her cheeks are completely wet. Vanesa sits up, clumsily hugs her little sister, and presses her tightly to her. Selīna doesn't resist, just pushes the computer aside, folds herself deeper into her sister's embrace, and releases her long-restrained sobs. Vanesa rocks her sister back and forth and lets her cry everything that's impossible to cry out. The thin jacket on Vanesa's shoulder quickly soaks through with Selīna's tears, they sit holding and don't say anything. Selīna's sobs and whimpers mix with the desperate howling of the blizzard behind the window. And what's there to talk about or say? They both know that the only escape from constant, unending despair would be to lose your mind and forget everything. All of it. Or die.

She has no idea how long they'd been sitting like that; Selīna finally calms down, and Vanesa realizes that it's getting dark outside. She hugs her sister tightly one more time and gets up to collect her things and drive home. It's too hard here, but she already knew that when she was driving over. She realizes that every year on this date.

Even with her arm injured, mom has already washed all the dishes. There are dishes and trays on the kitchen table with remains from this year's celebration. There's almost as much food as there was before the party. Vanesa feels anger and disgust rise from her solar plexus again, but doesn't say anything, she gets her purse and the shopping bags, declines her mother's offer of a doggy bag filled with today's leftovers, puts on her coat, and goes outside. She doesn't see the old man anywhere, he's either sleeping off the liquor or watching TV, but Vanesa doesn't have the slightest desire to look for him to say goodbye. Selīna and Gorodvojs walk with her as far as the veranda, they want to keep going, but Vanesa hugs her sister again and says goodbye right there. Outside and in every direction the snow whips around so much that it's impossible to see through it. Vanesa wraps her ears and chin tightly in her long, fluffy scarf, tosses her hood over her head, and wades through the snow toward the shed. The snow is getting deeper. For a moment Gorodvojs trudges alongside her, but then turns around and follows his own footsteps back. Soon the snow is above her boots. Reaching the Fiat, Vanesa feels crestfallen. The little red car is snowed in up to its windows, and the space in front of the shed is filled with snow; to get out, she'd need to dig out a path all the way to the main road. Vanesa wades in the direction of the road where snowdrifts— their tops sliced off by the wind—stretch sideways across it. Some patches of the road are bare, but it's clear that digging with a shovel, the work would take several hours . . . The blizzard doesn't relent . . .

Selīna is still standing on the veranda, waiting for her sister's car to drive out of the yard, to keep staring as she drives off into the distance. But the sound of the engine doesn't come, instead her sister walks back, steps onto the veranda, knocks the snow from her warm winter boots, brushes off her coat with her gloves, then takes off her hood.

"I'm snowed in. I won't be able to get out, it'll be dark soon anyway," Vanesa says.

Her anger starts to congeal into bitter phlegm at the back of her throat. To hell with it . . .

Mom looks confused, Vanesa never, not even once, has spent the night at "Rietumi," since she moved to the city after school. The old man has wandered back into the kitchen and is sitting in front of a full glass of liquor and a nearly empty bottle and, smiling happily, is crunching on some of the snacks from earlier. All that's missing is singing, then this "party" would be complete.

"I'll have to spend the night here. I'm snowed in, if I start digging, I won't finish before dark anyway. And the blizzard isn't letting up."

"I need to look where the old folding bed is. Haven't needed it in forever."

Mom finishes wiping off the empty spaces on the table with a rag.

"Don't worry about it! I'll just sleep in Dāvids's bed, it's already made."

Vanesa realizes what she's saying. The old man's glass halts just as he's about to take drink, and he puts it back down, and his mouth—lips already puckered toward the glass—remains open. Selīna slips quietly into her room. Her mother turns on the tap and spends a long time rinsing the rag she had used to wipe down the table. She had always, as much as she could, been orderly and tidy, even during those days when she couldn't tell morning from night.

"Gints, I think that cot is up in the attic to the left of the stairs. Climb up and bring it down to Selīna's room. And the mattress, it should be there too. Wrapped up and tied with some string."

"Mom, I said I'll sleep in Dāvids's room. Why move things around if there's no need? Why do you want to make me sleep on that old aluminum piece of junk in Selīna's tiny room if there's an empty room in the house with all that I need?"

The old man is still sitting motionless at the table. He closes his mouth though.

"No, you won't sleep there. That's Dāvids's room," Mom says a bit more quietly than before, but her words strike as sharply as the twisting snow hitting the windowpane.

Vanesa, though, isn't about to indulge her by agreeing and giving in without protest. It might be that the time has finally come to start chipping away at the wall of silence constructed over the last seven years.

"Mom, Dāvids is gone. And there are only two possibilities—either he wanted to run away from you so that no one would ever be able to find him, or he's dead. One way or another, he won't need that room or that bed."

"Dāvids isn't dead!"

"Even worse for you two! If he's alive and doesn't want to come back, who's fault is that, I wonder?"

Vanesa feels that black phlegm saturated with her anger and disgust gushing out from her in all directions.

"This old fool who crippled his face, or loving Mommy who was passed out drunk while it all happened? And not just that time. Do you remember how Dāvids left? Do you even remember the last time you saw him? Or the words, the last words you said to him? Do you even remember what Dāvids looked like?

Before the old man damaged his nerves and what he looked like afterward? Now it's all cakes and Cokes and chips, but when Dāvids really needed you . . ."

Behind her she hears a fist slamming against the wooden table. The dishes jump and fall back down with a clatter.

"Shut up, girl! Shut up! Or I'll . . ."

The old man hits the table again, everything rattles and shakes. But he doesn't say anything else. Clutching the neck of the nearly empty bottle in his fist, he stumbles out of the kitchen, hissing and wheezing through pinched lips. Vanesa doesn't feel afraid. She only feels the anger lodged in her throat and swelling in size, with no other way to escape than to spit it out so she doesn't choke and suffocate on it.

She turns and walks toward Dāvids's room. When did her mother find the time to wash even the floor with her sprained hand? She puts her bag down on the chair, takes off her coat, throws it over the backrest, collapses on the bed, and curls up into a ball. She presses her cheek against the pillow, closes her eyes, and empties her mind. Dāvids isn't here. Not the stubborn, thirteen-year-old boy with a damaged facial nerve who threw his bag over his shoulder one Saturday afternoon and changed all of their lives forever, not the twenty-year-old who still visits her but only in dreams and visions.

August 14, 2014

My last year of school starts in two weeks. I don't know what to do next, I don't have enough brains or energy for university. I'll need to find a job. There's no way I'm sticking around here. If I'd known that Mom would stop drinking, that the old man would calm down, and that Selīna would be safe at home, I wouldn't have quit that program. I regret that so, so much. But I couldn't have known. How often would we have made a different choice, if only we had known . . . if we had predicted or sensed what would happen.

There's no point studying gardening anymore, a waste of time. I'll look for a job. The whole school year is still ahead of me, I'll think about it, look at wanted ads. I'm sure I'll find my way. I'm sure of it.

In the beginning of July, some kids found a body in the forest outside of town. In a ditch right by the roots of a spruce tree. Already pretty decomposed, there wasn't much left of the clothes. Mom had to go and look at them, but she couldn't see any part of Dāvids's clothes in those rotting rags. Then they did a DNA test. It wasn't Dāvids. I can't tell anyone else, but I hoped it would be him. So he'd get a real funeral, so we could have a good cry, so he'd finally be buried forever, so he'd had a normal coffin and grave, not that memorial vault inside of our house. Almost two years have gone by, Mom still doesn't let anyone go into Dāvids's room, let alone change or reorganize even the tiniest thing. If he had died, I could move into his room. I'm tired of the waiting, the uncertainty, the mourning and not being allowed to mourn. Sometime and somehow, it's got to end. Two years—that's way too long to keep trying to stay strong and not to crack even a tiny, little bit . . .

Vanesa hears her mother come into the room, but she doesn't turn around or open her eyes, and hopes that the instinctive tensing of her muscles won't be noticeable. Her mother sits down in the chair and is quiet for a moment. Vanesa despises her. Her mother and whatever words she is going to say next, dripping with excuses and accusations.

"Vanesa, I want . . . I don't know how . . . Just listen to me. We've never had the chance to talk . . . Or, actually, I never had the courage to start the conversation. Maybe I felt like you wouldn't want to listen anyway. You'll think that I'm looking for excuses for myself or trying to make you feel sorry for me. Understand that I really don't need that, honestly, no, that would be stupid. I can't have it anyway. I wanted to tell you how I've got no right to live. And no right to die. I wonder if you've ever thought about how painstakingly and cruelly my own sins are taking their revenge on me now . . . And how painstaking and cruel I sometimes plan my own death to be."

Vanesa feels her body relax, she opens her eyes and turns toward her mother, but still doesn't get up from the bed. Mom is sitting there completely calm, her hands set one atop the other on her lap, her head bent slightly as she speaks.

"Do I deserve death? As a punishment or as a gift? To die with the greatest suffering, experiencing unbearable pain . . . That would be fair, yes, that's what I deserve, but that would save me from the suffering I have to live with every day, every minute, since Dāvids disappeared. Death—that would be easier . . . Do I deserve something that's easier than this life? This absolutely pointless life and its sole purpose to experience suffering . . . Suffering as a punishment that I have to endure. With no chance of a reprieve."

Vanesa is about to open her mouth, to say something, to object, to convince, but the words don't come to her, and her mouth remains closed. Her mom's words are unexpected, heavy, and painful, maybe Vanesa had sometimes tried to imagine what her mom feels, how she copes, what she thinks, what demons she struggles with; how to ask her, how to start a conversation if nobody has ever asked anyone else in their family—how do you feel, what's wrong, what do you want? Even back when Dāvids was still a small, sweet boy with a smile stretching across his whole face . . .

"Mom, why did you start drinking?" The unexpected question surprises Vanesa. As if the answer would change anything, to drive away the dark, sticky fog hanging over this house and its residents, who have already spent years wandering around inside of it, without touching or even really seeing each other.

Her mother is quiet for a moment.

"I don't know. I've got no answer. Whatever I'd say, whatever I'd give as the reason, that would be an attempt to lessen my guilt. And anyway it wouldn't be true. I just drank. Out of carelessness, stupidity, neglect."

"But Gints . . ."

"No, don't blame Gints for my drinking. How many wives suffer with alcoholic husbands, but keep it together, live, work, and take care of the house and kids. Gints is to blame for his own drinking, nobody else but me is to blame for mine."

She stops talking again, runs her hand over her aching shoulder, then continues:

"However much it's possible to screw up your own life, I've done exactly that. Almost on purpose, almost as if to spite myself. And there's no chance of fixing anything."

"Why do you keep this room like this? Fine, a minute ago I was too harsh, but still—if Dāvids ever comes back, I doubt that he'd want to return to exactly where he ran away from. He grew out of those clothes long ago . . . And those school books . . . You do it so that every day you can hurt yourself all over again?

"Not just yourself but also the rest of us. You know, I hate two days out of the year—Dāvids's birthday and that Saturday in September . . . I wanted to tell you a long time ago, but just couldn't work up the courage. I'm not coming anymore. I feel like this is a parody, the party and sitting at the table, the cake, chips, and Coke. It's like a mockery. You can all do what you want."

The blizzard is still raging outside, whistling and howling, but the room feels peaceful at last. Someone opens the door, slowly, carefully. First, a large, furry paw, then a nose presses in through the gap between the door and its frame, and Gorodvojs lumbers into the room. His nails scratching against the floorboards, he walks over to Mom and lies down, pressing against her leg. Vanesa's mother is deep in thought, it seems like she doesn't even notice how she ruffles the dog's shaggy ears and strokes his large, graying head. Gorodvojs closes his eyes and rests his head on his paws.

"I'll know," Mom finally says, "When the time is right."

They'd never spoken so much or so openly. Maybe when Vanesa was a child, but she can't remember that. She wants to ask more questions. Why doesn't Mom kick Gints out, why are they still together. Why does she let Selīna sink deeper into solitude and lose herself in the virtual world. Vanesa has invited her sister over, but Mom is always the first to cancel, saying that Selīna isn't used to leaving the house and doesn't even go anywhere around here, let alone to the city . . . Maybe they'll talk again sometime. Tonight Vanesa is tired.

Mom doesn't say anything else, she ruffles the back of the dog's head one more time and quietly leaves the room. Selīna and the old man must be watching some show in the TV room. Jingles, unnatural canned laughter, and applause. The overly sunny tone of the host's voice, even without being able to make out the words, sounds almost like anguished screams.

"How annoying," Vanesa thinks and suddenly remembers Rihards.

He's probably called. She digs her phone out of her purse, flips open its cover, and—yes. Four unanswered calls and two text messages.

"I've had enough drama tonight," Vanesa decides and, without reading anything, mutes the phone and puts it back in her purse.

Strange, she thinks to herself, as she realizes that she doesn't care about not seeing Rihards today and doesn't miss him at all . . . Even though he's a caring and passionate lover, and remembering the touch of his lips and fingers brings warmth rushing to her cheeks and crotch, being with Rihards makes her feel even more alone than when she's actually alone during her daily rush . . .

It always feels like a missed train. And that feeling never changes.

That's it, Vanesa is going to sleep. She opens the door, loudly calls out "Good night!," gets undressed, and crawls under the blanket on her brother's bed. Her head feels heavy on the pillow, it's been a very exhausting day. The blizzard is still going wild outside, whistling, roaring, driving fistfuls of snow into the windows, but they're sealed well and the stoves are heated piping hot. There's just that unpleasant smell. Earlier, during the birthday meal, it was just barely noticeable, now it's gradually filling the room like the black phlegm she'd felt during the day, permeated by her anger expanding, bulging, and rising up higher and higher in her body. She feels very tired, but the stench of decay keeps getting stronger, it overwhelms the fresh smell of the bed sheets, it's hard to breathe, it presses on her chest and scares her. Why, where is it coming from? Vanesa shifts from one side to the other, trying to stick her head under the blanket, so she doesn't smell it, then pulls her head out again and sleeps with her nose in the pillow. Nothing helps. Fine, she thinks, let it be, let it stink. She lies down on her back, relaxes, and breathes freely, she knows that like other times, as she gets used to it, eventually she won't notice the stench at all, surely it'll fade this time too . . .

No. She can't take it anymore. Vanesa gets up quietly and goes over to one of the two windows in the room. Mom pastes paper strips onto the window frame using laundry soap moistened with water, it's cheap, holds up well, and is easy to wash off in the spring with warm water. Vanesa scratches at one of the strips and tugs at it, it doesn't come off easily at all, but there's nothing left to breathe, her chest feels like a barrel bound tightly by hoops and she's afraid that any second now she'll erupt with a roaring, barking cough, and that then everyone will run in here, run to see what's wrong with her, no, she doesn't want that. She twists open the window handle, she yanks the window toward her, and with a gentle zip the paper strips tear in half. She still has to do the same to the other one, these aren't plastic pre-fab windows, these are sturdy Soviet-era double windows with wooden frames. Vanesa pushes open the outer window the same way, it swings out, and the blizzard's racing winds tear into the room, throwing open the window all the way to the wall, knocking down the red cyclamen, sealing up her eyes, scattering snow all over the floor, lifting up everything on the table and spinning it around in a whirlwind, papers, books, it snatches the clothes Vanesa had placed on the chair, the vortex is getting bigger and more savage, now and then launching something out the window. Dāvids's photograph flies away, then Vanesa's purse, then the whirlwind throws open the closet doors, Dāvids's jeans, T-shirts, laundry are all whisked away, she tries to force the window closed again, but she can't, the wind tears it from her hands and slams it against the outer wall with a loud thud, it shatters with a tinkling sound into countless tiny shards, which are lifted up in an instant and swirl into the tornado spinning around the room. The wind throws everything, absolutely everything outside and carries it off, nothing remains that could suggest that Dāvids had ever lived there . . . Vanesa is terrified, no one is coming to save her, do they really not hear what's happening, and finally she cries out:

"Help, come help me!"

She's surprised by her own cry. Her eyes are still sealed shut, but the air in the room seems clean and cool . . . Vanesa breathes in several times through her nose. No hint of decay or any other kind of rancid smell. The house is quiet. She doesn't hear the TV or conversations, everyone is probably sleeping. And outside the window it's also finally quiet. Her unease doesn't leave her right away, but Vanesa is able gradually to relax and open her eyes. In the room, everything is sitting where it was, nothing has been thrown about or even moved from its place. She gets up quietly and walks to the window. The clouds have almost completely cleared, an occasional gray strand scurries across the sparkling, smirking face of the moon. Snow drifts cover the yard, Vanesa presses her forehead against the windowpane, but can't see the spot where her car is parked, just the very end of the barn. From there to the driveway someone has cleared a narrow path.

"It has to be the fox," Vanesa thinks to herself, smiles, and crawls back under the blanket.

Retreating to warmth, she falls asleep in an instant, this time her sleep is deep and dreamless.

Vanesa wakes up early and for a moment she doesn't know where she is. Outside the window it's still dark, it's not clear if it's the middle of the night or morning. She looks at her phone screen. Six-thirty. And four text messages. Something has changed, she feels a sense of alienation and dislike toward Rihards. The messages remain unread. Vanesa stretches and crawls out of bed. The floor is cold, the room has cooled over-night; she gets dressed quickly and throws her warm scarf over her shoulders. Most of all she'd like to slip out and drive away without anyone noticing. But she has to dig the car out of the snow and it's clear that she won't be able to do that with-out making some noise. Vanesa listens. The house is still quiet. Mom won't be going to work today, because of her sprained arm. Hopefully, she's still asleep . . .

She quietly puts her things into her bag and tries to open the bedroom door without making a sound. It works. But a light is shining across the front hall through the narrow gap of the open kitchen door . . . Vanesa sighs and heads toward it. Mom is sitting by the lit oven, on the table is a plate where she has cut up some cucumber and arranged slices of bread with cheese along with a small piece of yesterday's cake on a saucer.

"I've got breakfast for you here . . ." she says seeing her daughter standing in the doorway. "The water is hot, if you want coffee, I'll put it on so it boils."

"You've only got instant coffee here, right?"

"Does this work?"

Mom pulls a small, unopened pack of ground Jacobs coffee from deep inside the upper cabinet.

"That'll work. I'll have a bite to eat and then go dig out the car." Her mom pushes the water kettle onto the heating rings, then turns around and says:

"Gints already dug it out during the night when the blizzard died down. He couldn't sleep, you know how it is when he's been drinking, he can't relax . . . He dug a path out to the road, you'll be able to drive out right away. He's in bed now, after that hard work he was finally able to fall asleep.

Vanesa takes a bite of bread with cheese and feels a tear run down her cheek. She can't understand anything in this place or make sense of it enough to at least know who is good or bad, whom she should hate or love. Whom should she blame or comfort and how should she deal with her constant feelings of guilt.

"How's your shoulder this morning?" Vanesa asks as she pours boiling water into her coffee cup.

"I'll manage, yesterday I rubbed it with some liquor, I stole a shot from Gints's bottle," Mom smiles, "it's a miracle he didn't even notice."

Vanesa laughs.

"Mom, remember when I moved to the city, I put everything that I couldn't take with me into a largeish plywood box. Do you have any idea where it could be?"

"I think it's upstairs, in that storage space."

"I'll go up there and take a look, I won't take the whole box with me yet, just . . . I'll be back next month. Maybe talk to Selīna, she could spend a day or two with me during her school break."

Her mom doesn't say anything, just nods.

Vanesa climbs up to the attic and, yes, behind the folding bed and mattress are two old suitcases—who knows anymore if empty or full—and next to them a box. At the top there's a photo album, a few CDs, further down there are gifts from classmates, memorabilia, books with signatures. At the bottom there is a plain-looking spiral notebook. Vanesa pulls it out, shakes it, dust and webs stick to her hands and clothes. Then she puts everything else back into the box and climbs downstairs.

July 25, 2015

I'm done. I finished school. I won't say it was perfect, but also not that bad, about what I expected. On average 6.1. My exam results were okay—a C level, a B in Latvian, but it doesn't matter, I'm not applying to university. I've planned it all out. I'm leaving, I'm going to work at a nursery school. That'll only be for a while. I'll take business administration courses at night, I already applied, and then I'll find work as a secretary. I found a room to live in, fairly cheap, the kitchen and bathroom are shared, there'll be some other student in the other room come September, but I don't care. I'm heading to the city the day after tomorrow. I know that it'll all work out, I've always known how to make it work and get things done without anyone else's help. If I need it, I can also help others.

I won't have to look at my mother's stony face and keep thinking all the time about what I can and can't say, what will hurt her, what will annoy her, as if I didn't have my own reasons to hurt or be angry. But can I show it? I want to get away from everything, maybe that's the same thing that Dāvids wanted. Maybe, or maybe not. I don't know. Probably not though. Dāvids ran away out of spite, he wanted to show that he was stronger than the old man, than the mess in our house, that he was stronger than fate. And he succeeded. He shattered everything that had been here up until then and turned it on its head. But I'm running away because I'm weak . . . I don't have the power to change anything here. I don't have the strength to wait and believe, because I don't believe anymore . . . I want a different life, one where the things that actually exist matter instead of those that don't. I know what I'm writing is awful, but I want to live without Dāvids's ghost from now on, and that just can't happen here at "Rietumi". I just want to live my life. My own life. I don't know if it'll work out for me, but I'll do whatever I can, so I can truly get away. Nothing is going to change here . . .

I know that Dāvids would understand me. Just like I understand him.

This morning there's a light frost, the sky is completely clear and fresh, glittering snow dazzles her eyes to tears. Vanesa hadn't brought her sunglasses, and the morning sun is much too low for the visor in her car to do much good. She drives slowly on the snowy road, glancing now and again over at the blanket of snow, which forest animals have already decorated with the crisscross path of their footprints. The roadside ditches are filled with drifts, but the road is relatively smooth and bare, the wind having wiped the snow across it. Nobody will be plowing this road before tomorrow—it's Sunday. It'll be lucky if they plow the more important roads. But almost no one drives on this one, it's still some three kilometers to the main road.

And then she notices a white car stuck in a drift in the roadside ditch and a man standing next to it who is motioning, asking her to stop. Vanesa recoils instinctively and almost steps on the gas to drive past faster, then rebukes herself. Nobody else is going to pass by here. Nobody else will help. And so she stops her car next to the Audi stuck in the ditch. The man walks around her car and leans down toward her window. She presses the button and the window slides down.

"Good morning, it's lucky you were driving by. Can you help me? I need to get to the guesthouse just past this patch of forest."

He gestures; Vanesa knows that guesthouse.

"Can you take me? It's about seven kilometers, maybe it's even on your way?"

It's not really on Vanesa's way, but it would be only two-and-a-half kilometers off her route. But she still hesitates. Why didn't he ask her to help pull his car out? Vanesa doesn't have a cable in her trunk, but he doesn't even ask. And what about him? Doesn't he have one?

"I can't even call, my phone is dead."

"I can give you mine," Vanesa finally says something.

"Does anybody even know a phone number off the top of their head these days?"

The man laughs.

His laughter is bright like the morning, light, disarming, and Vanesa opens the passenger-side door.

"Get in, I'll take you."

The man walks over to his Audi one more time, grabs his bag, slams the door shut, and when he's already sitting in Vanesa's car, he locks it with the key fob.

"A fox ran out in front of me, I didn't want to hit it so I swerved, and here I am," he explains even though Vanesa hadn't asked.

She also doesn't want to talk to this stranger, so she turns on the radio. A joyful Sunday morning melody flows together with the glittering, white landscape outside the car windows, and she gently accelerates.

A straight nose, its end flat with a small, shallow indentation. Narrow nostrils. Very short, graying stubble, but a classic haircut without a single strand of white, just typical Latvian gray. Blue eyes, squinting slightly, bags under them. A small vertical scar above his right eyebrow. His eyebrows are straight, thin. His hands are clean, groomed, his fingers are massive, stubby, their first joints are a bit hairy, no ring. About forty, maybe a bit more. Black dress pants, hastily pressed but clean, a warm, dark blue overcoat, a black scarf, his shoes don't really match the rest—red-white-blue warm hiking boots. A gray bag with a gray strap, with many exterior pockets and compartments, it looks fairly heavy. The man is holding the bag in his lap, shifting it every now and again, and it seems to Vanesa that any moment now he'll take out a Coke bottle so he can take a drink with a disgusting gulp.

The Audi's license plate had sunk into the snow and wasn't visible.

Vanesa has learned how to notice absolutely everything even without looking directly at it. She hadn't learned to do it yet when she needed it the most.

The sunny melody ends and the next song begins. A furious rhythm and heart-wrenching guitar, the voice and lyrics filled with despair. This time Vanesa doesn't change the station. It seems no one can help me now . . .

"It's strange that this song is playing," the man says. "Have you seen the video?"

Vanesa doesn't answer.

"I only mention it because the video is about children who disappeared and were never found. And right here some years ago there was a boy who disappeared, maybe you've heard about it. They never found him. A strange coincidence, whenever I drive here, I always think about that case, and now this song . . ."

Bought a ticket for a runaway train

Like a madman laughing at the rain . . .

"Yes," Vanesa says, "I know. It's by Soul Asylum."

The car slowly rolls to a stop by a stand of fir trees planted in front of the guesthouse.

"Thanks and safe travels," the man says, as he smiles at Vanesa, gets out of the Fiat, throws his bag over his shoulder, and heads toward the building's main entrance.

BIRTHDAY

"A-four," Karolīna says as she hides her piece of graph paper behind her backpack.

"Miss. T-seven," Sergejs whispers ominously, but his eyes are squinting from a smile.

"Hit," Karolīna answers with barely concealed annoyance.

"T-eight."

"Hit."

Karolīna glances over suspiciously at Sergejs, judging the distance between them and the angle of his gaze.

"You're peeking," she hisses angrily.

Sergejs laughs. He lowers himself so he's partially stretched out on the sharp dune grass and supports himself on one elbow, as he holds onto the wind-ruffled page; he colors in the T-8 square to mark a hit by his ship.

"U-eight," he says with a winner's confidence.

"Sunk . . ."

Karolīna sounds very grumpy.

"I don't want to play anymore, you keep winning all the time anyway. Peeker!"

"Fine, if you don't want to, then let's not play," Sergejs doesn't even object.

Without getting up, he rolls over to Karolīna and, hugging her with both arms, pulls her down so she's lying next to him. Karolīna resists a bit just for appearances, but a moment later rests her head against Sergejs's strong, muscular upper arms and lets him take her hand into his. Sergejs intertwines his powerful fingers with her slender ones, and they lie together like that, staring at the sky. Wispy clouds spread across it crisscrossed by white airplane contrails. The sea sighs gently beyond the dunes, calmly tossing one wave over another and that wave over a third, and on and on. Perfect weather for a hike, Karolīna thinks to herself amid feelings of comfort and relaxation.

"It looks like it's going to rain tomorrow," Sergejs says, staring at the sky.

"What do you mean—rain?" Karolīna asks anxiously. "It's such good hiking weather. We don't need any need rain!"

"Those clouds show that the weather is changing."

He points at the translucent, feathery white clouds.

"If it rains, are we going to keep going?"

"We can do what you want. We can spend the whole day in the tent, I've got a waterproof one, 3000mm. We'll sleep, make love."

Karolīna doesn't have the slightest idea what "3000mm" means. And making love in a tent seems just in general off to her. She needs a shower before and after, a wide bed with soft, smooth satin sheets, and a glass of cool wine right after the shower.

"Well, shall we keep going?" Sergejs asks after a brief silence.

Without answering, Karolīna gets up, her knees are already tired from walking, they ache. Well, yeah, she's not thirty or even fifty anymore. She's fifty-six. Karolīna gathers up their sandwich wrappers, a water bottle, and a pad of graph paper, and puts her backpack on her back.

The hike was Sergejs's idea.

"Three days along the coast and fifty-eight kilometers, it's like pissing on two fingers," he said.

Karolīna doesn't pee on her fingers, she doesn't know what kind of measure of ease or difficulty that is. At first he'd wanted to walk eighty kilometers, also in three days. Totally crazy. Of course, for him that would be equivalent to peeing on one finger, but for Karolīna this is the first three-day hike of her life, she even had to ask for Friday off. She's not sure about the fifty-eight either. And now the clouds are promising rain, too. Maybe she shouldn't have come, it would have been nice to relax over the weekend, there's the Anna's Day market in Rožu Square and, in the evening, the group Raxtu raxti is performing in Čakste Square, but tomorrow night Artis is playing his red saxophone over at the beachside cafe Vēju dārzs. At least she could've enjoyed some culture, instead of wandering across the dunes with this half-crazed braggart and sand crunching between her teeth the whole time. Sergejs is a seasoned wanderer, he's cycled all over Europe, rowed down rivers, walked across mountains. As much as Karolīna can understand, he's not quite a mountaineer, he doesn't climb mountains using special equipment—that's all she needs—but he has walked all through the Alps, the Tatras, and some other place too, Karolīna can't keep track of it all.

They walk fifteen kilometers in four hours. They'd started at the Lithuanian border and gone through the coastal villages of Nida and Pape. Karolīna immediately settles into her usual, measured, natural gait, he better not even hope that she'll trot alongside him at his pace. That's how they walked, Sergejs constantly going faster, gradually moving off into the distance, then coming back to her, walking alongside her for a moment, then moving off into the distance again.

"You'll definitely walk all eighty of those kilometers you'd wanted," Karolīna chuckles.

The smartwatch with the step counter and distance meter is only around Sergejs's wrist, and the levels it shows won't have the slightest connection with what Karolīna will have walked or the calories she will have burned along the way. The tent is on Sergejs's back, as is the kettle for boiling water, Karolīna just has some warmer clothes for nighttime, a first-aid kit, a water bottle that she needs to fill up somewhere along the way, and rolled up sleeping pads tied to her bag, but they don't weigh anything anyway. There were also a couple sandwiches, but they had just eaten those, she didn't bring more, over three days they'd just spoil, the weather is hot. Sergejs promised to take care of the food.

On the beach in Nida, a group of men is milling around a boat and tractor, shoving and yelling:

"*Kartu! Kartu! Irkla, imk irkla!*" It's not working, davai, push!

The tractor drives into the sea and, with the men pushing from the back, it pulls the boat into the water. Four of the pushers jump into the boat and row right out to sea, the others watch for a moment, then slowly wade back to shore.

"They're fishing," Sergejs intones knowingly. "It's like a paid adventure for them here, you catch your own fish, pull the nets out on your own, then smoke and eat them right here."

He motions toward two reed roofs behind the dunes.

"A local guy, he and his wife make good money, keeping a boat, nets, a tractor, and a smokehouse."

Karolīna isn't especially interested, though she'd be pretty agreeable to picking apart a hot, freshly smoked flounder. She finds her pace and keeps walking calmly just like before, not saying very much. Trudging through sand demands more effort than walking on the city's cobblestones, she could always climb down from the dune, walk right along the edge of the beach, but along this stretch, the sand is completely covered with pebbles and sea detritus, and walking on that is even harder.

"Let's go on a hike," he said. "You'll see, it'll give our relationship a different perspective, a new dimension. Like freshening your breath."

Karolīna just smirks, thinking to herself, "I've already got fresh breath." The adventure was kind of tempting, kind of not. Just like Sergejs.

"Let's get married," he said after his first night in her bed.

"You're deranged," she answered.

He hummed Mendelssohn's "Wedding March" while blowing a raspberry. Then they both laughed for a long time until they started making love again.

Karolīna trudges down the sandy trail along the top of the dunes; Sergejs has moved off again. Only his gray backpack with its bright green trim is visible ahead. Suddenly he stops, looks back, and starts waving his arms. Karolīna doesn't speed up, but walks calmly at the same pace. When she gets closer to Sergejs, he starts gesturing emphatically for her to approach quietly—his index finger on his lips and an enthusiastic expression on his face. He is hushing her with one hand, and motioning toward the bushes down below the dune with the other. Karolīna notices the posts and crossbeams of a paddock on the edge of the bushes, but doesn't yet see what Sergejs is so enthusiastically trying to draw her attention to. And then she sees it, lying on the brown rocks, a herd of big hunchbacked cows, with flat foreheads and pointed horns curving forward. In the middle of the herd she catches sight of smaller, brown-furred mounds, some extremely small and unremarkable. She walks up very close to Sergejs and grabs his hand fearfully.

"Bison. Be quiet, these guys are insanely aggressive and bloodthirsty, they can attack if they're woken up," Sergejs whispers into her ear.

"Maybe we should get out of here?" Karolīna whispers back, frightened out of her wits as she presses closer to him.

"No, I want to see what happens when they notice us."

Sergejs puts his arm around Karolīna and starts speaking.

"Ohoo! Ohoho!" he calls out the bison, but not very loudly.

Karolīna's heart is in her throat, she is ready to flee alone, down the dune and out to the beach. Those creatures are beautiful, but even when asleep they look humongous, any second now they'll get up, and then there'll be trouble. But Sergejs, sensing Karolīna's desire to run away, holds her in a tight embrace.

"Oho, oho!"

He tries to attract the attention of the bison. One cow gets up and stares blankly in their direction.

"Let's run before it's too late!" Karolīna tries desperately to convince Sergejs, but he starts to laugh.

"Stop it. I'm just bullshitting, they're as peaceful as pillows, they're a hundred times more frightened of us than we are of them. See how sleepy they are, and those are only cows with calves. Look, what a little sweetheart."

In the meantime, one of the tiny mounds has also gotten up, a very small calf, and stands next to the large she-bison, and stares at them in exactly the same blank way. Then it walks up to the cow and pokes her flank with its nose.

"If there were bulls here too, then we would need to be more careful. The bulls can weigh as much as nine hundred kilograms, the cows are light—five hundred, maybe six hundred, some even less. Bison live apart from each other, there's a bull herd and a cow herd with the calves. Toward the end of the summer, the bulls start needing their women, and then all of the bison spend some time living together. Supposedly they start mating in late July, but, look, there aren't bulls here yet. When all of the cows have been impregnated, the bulls leave again in October—to their own herd, their own life. Well, you know, men have men's work."

Karolīna shoves her elbow into Sergejs's side. She's still a bit afraid, but clearly the she-bison are not particularly interested in people. Karolīna wants to photograph these hunchbacked brown cows, but they had both turned off their phones and stuck them into the depths of their bags.

"In case there's an emergency, otherwise we could just leave them behind," Sergejs had announced without hesitation before the hike.

It had also seemed like exciting to Karolīna, a good challenge—three days, existing only in the "here and now."

"There should be wild horses too," Sergejs keeps talking as he looks around. "But these paddocks are immense, we might not see them at all. But this was really lucky, there aren't a lot of bison, and their trails are impossible to make out."

"Amen," Karolīna declares. "Should we keep going?"

"Are you going to marry me?" he asks with exaggerated seriousness, as if it were all dependent on her answer.

"Clown," Karolīna says playfully and goes to climb down the dune. There are no pebbles on the beach anymore and it'll be easier to walk for a while down the wave-flattened shore.

It's a good thing that she had put on her worn-in sneakers after all, not the new, white ones. The old leather shoes have stretched from being worn and perfectly fit her foot, which over the years has grown too wide for its small size. She'd wanted to look attractive and elegant next to youthful Sergejs, but in the end it was either attractive, modern, and unworn shoes with a face twisted in agony or old shoes that she could just completely forget about with freedom and the joy of movement in her body and face. Karolīna fortunately chose the second option. She trudges over to the beach's clearing and its tightly-packed sand smoothed by the water, and now her steps are so light she is practically flying. Sergejs watches the bison for a moment longer then hesitates as he climbs down, but soon he is again a good distance ahead of Karolīna.

The sun is already sitting just above the sea, and Karolīna can't really feel her feet anymore. No, nothing hurts, there's just a stiffness that's gotten into them, she's not used to walking such long distances, and trudging through the sand a while ago required more effort than planned. The next time that Sergejs waits for her or turns around toward her, Karolīna will say that she doesn't want to go any further today. After all, she doesn't have to compete or prove anything to anyone. If she can't go any further, then she doesn't have to. Behind the dunes there is a tiny, slanted pine forest, the constant west wind has bent it away from the sea. She doesn't know where Sergejs has planned for them to camp that night.

Sergejs has stopped and is squatting down behind a knobby dead log studying something in the sand. Karolīna feels like she is using up her final strength to keep up with him, but catching sight of what he's studying, she practically jumps in the air and screams, springing back to a safe distance. A large, black snake is twisting and winding into loops and knots, opening and closing its mouth, baring its sharp fangs, and using its forked tongue to threaten Sergejs who is using a sea-smoothed piece of wood to keep it at a distance.

"Why are you yelling like crazy, it's just a grass snake. Just look at the size, I've never seen a giant like that before."

"Just a grass snake, but you're still shaking that little stick at it," Karolīna shoots back angrily.

"Well, he can bite, just like any snake. Look at his mouth, at his fangs. But there's no venom there. What a beauty," Sergejs gushes.

"Sergejs, I'm done. I can't go any further today."

"That's fine, sweetheart. We're here, anyway." He leaves the snake alone and it soon crawls behind the dead log and slithers away across the sand leaving a flowing zig-zag trail in its wake.

Sergejs walks over and hugs Karolīna. She gives in and leans against him as they both stand there together for a moment. That turns out to be good and relaxing, and when Sergejs finally takes her by the hand, Karolīna feels that she can walk again. Or at least far enough to reach the spot where Sergejs had wanted to set up the tent. They climb up the dune, behind it is a forest path leading into the pine grove. Bentgrass and bilberry bushes scrape her legs as they walk down the path into the forest.

"Do you think there are ticks here?" Karolīna mentions worriedly.

"If you can convince yourself that there aren't, and that they won't get you, then there won't be any even if there are."

"Fine," Karolīna agrees, not understanding Sergejs's logic.

After a three-minute walk, the path leads out into a small, sunny meadow. This will be the spot for the tent. Karolīna likes it a lot, and the sea is really close, they'll be able to watch the sunset and go for a swim before nightfall. And then she notices an enclosure made of piled stones, and beyond them the wooden crosses and black, polished granite monuments.

"Sergejs! Sergejs, come on, stop, we're not setting up our tent here!" she is practically yelling.

"Shush, don't yell! Don't disturb the sleepers! When you're sleeping, you'll want it to be quiet too."

Sergejs calmly takes the bag and tent off his back, puts them down, and starts unpacking. Karolīna sits down on the grass and grabs her head. She's going to leave. If there is a graveyard here, that means that there must be some houses around here too, no way there is a cemetery all by itself in the forest. In the worst case she might have to walk to the highway, that can't be more than eight kilometers . . . Eight kilometers! No, she can't walk eight more kilometers, so she falls onto her back in the soft grass. A tear trickles down from the corner of her eye, but Karolīna doesn't whimper or sob.

"Was there really no better place?" she asks, her voice tinged with despair.

"This spot will be great, there's a well on the other side of the graveyard, and, look, there's even a spot for a fire, this must be where they burn the spruce branches that are taken off the graves in the spring," Sergejs points to a substantial blackened area fringed by large stones.

"Water from the graveyard well and a fire on top of the bones of corpses . . ."

Karolīna doesn't know whether to laugh or cry. In the meantime, Sergejs has already almost pitched the tent, thank God, at least it's outside of the graveyard . . .

"The water will get boiled. The corpse bones will stay where they are, just like ours."

"You promise?" Karolīna's voice has a dramatic tone.

"I swear on my life," Sergejs declares solemnly.

"Come on, stop it for once, my hair is already standing on end as it is."

"Really? In the light of day? What are you going to do at night?" he laughs, takes the kettle, and walks toward the cemetery. "I'll bring some water for tea."

"Wait, I'll come with you!" Karolīna scrambles upright and toddles after Sergejs.

The cemetery is well-tended. The grass is mowed. The grave mounds vary, fresh summer flowers have been planted on some, others are covered with ivy and houseleek, it's hard to tell if anyone has visited them this summer yet or not. Others are completely overgrown with grass. The wooden crosses are leaning to one side and covered with lichen. Karolīna looks over the cemetery enclosure in every direction to see if there are any houses nearby. It would be safer. But she doesn't see anything, just a wide gravel road leading away from the other side of the graveyard toward the forest.

Sergejs winds his way between the graves as if he were searching for something. Finally, he stops in front of a large, reddish stone and calls Karolīna over.

"Come here, I want to show you something."

Karolīna walks over. Sergejs is standing, his head bowed, by a stone with the inscription—"Klaušnieks." Below it—"Karolīna and Sergejs." There are years next to each of them.

"Those are my grandparents on my mother's side," Sergejs says quietly.

"Sergejs and Karolīna!" Karolīna gasps. "But you're from the southeast, from Krustpils—in Selonia! You never told me that your grandparents were from our neck of the woods."

"I was young, I didn't care. I'm telling you now though. I'm named in honor of my grandfather, you also never asked me why I, a pure Latvian, have such a Slavic name."

The gravel around both mounds is neatly raked, and by the stone there is a large clay pot of white and pink begonias.

"It's so well-tended. Do you still have any relatives living here?"

"I don't, but my grandfather's sister had a daughter—my mom's cousin. Her parents are also at rest somewhere in this cemetery, so then she probably also takes care of my granny and gramps at the same time. We don't have any contact with her."

"Strange to see the names—Karolīna and Sergejs—on the monument. At least the last name is different," Karolīna mutters. "We can take whatever last name we want when we get married." Karolīna doesn't even argue anymore, just snorts and turns around to leave. The well is completely covered with a lid and above it there is a canopy with a splint roof, but even so Karolīna thinks about the groundwater by the cemetery, about everything from the decaying coffins and their contents soaking into the surrounding soil. But she doesn't say anything else to Sergejs anymore, just promises herself only to drink or otherwise use water that's been boiled for at least ten minutes.

"How do you feel?" Sergejs asks when they're both in the tent, in the dark, each in their own sleeping bag, only their heads touching. "Are you sorry you agreed to come?"

"Not anymore," Karolīna answers frankly. "But when we were walking, I managed to regret it at least five times." They both laugh warmly. Karolīna's cheeks are burning, probably from the sea wind, because they mostly walked with their backs to the sun, and her knees ache. The evening swim has revived her body and loosened up her tired hips, but the fresh peppermint tea before bedtime has calmed her nervous system which had been oversaturated by impressions. For dinner Sergejs pulls out a container of freeze dried Rollton mashed potatoes, rye bread, and vacuum-packed salami. At first, before the potatoes had been reconstituted, Karolīna was turning up her nose, but when she started eating, she ate all of it and even carefully scraped out the last of the potatoes from their container. "Did you have a lot of men while I was wandering around, finding myself?" Sergejs pushes his sleeping bag closer.

"Wait, let me count . . ." Karolīna says and pauses. "Seventy-six or maybe seventy-seven, if you count those twins separately."

Sergejs pauses too, then starts laughing quietly, but affectionately.

"Were they Siamese twins?"

Now Karolīna is laughing too. She won't say, of course, how during that time she'd fallen unhappily in love again, that someone had left her again for somebody else, and that in general—it's a woman's fate to love and suffer, but now she has strongly resolved to cheat fate.

"But wasn't I your first love? Back then when we made love for the first time."

The first time she was eighteen. He was twenty-one. My god, it's been thirty-eight years! "No. Before that I already loved Gojko Mitić, after that Vladimir Konkin and Al Pacino. But I almost lost my mind because of Matangi."

"Holy crap, who is Matangi?" Sergejs can barely keep down his laughter.

"Matangi from the movie 'Hurricane', and don't ask me what the actor's name was, what country the movie was made in, I don't remember anything. But Matangi was half-naked with tousled hair, and wild, and I lost my mind."

Sergejs guffaws again.

"And I also need to tell you about the architect. I've been hiding him from you."

"About the architect . . . What else about the architect?"

"When I was in high school, I fell head over heels for some young man."

"Where did you meet him?"

"I didn't. I saw him on the street. No matter where I went, he nearly always showed up along the way. Imagine, the beginning of the eighties, everybody in identical gray jackets, knit hats, and those puffy winter boots that were in fashion back then, like fat caterpillars around your feet, but then all of a sudden—a young guy in a long, black coat with a white scarf and a black bowler hat and always wearing shined leather shoes. You couldn't ignore him! And always alone. Tall, gazing off into the distance, as if he were not of this world.

"And? You got to know each other?"

"No, stop it. There are people who you don't need to get to know. And how could I get to know him if he walked around as if he didn't see anybody."

"How do you know then that he was an architect?"

"He was always holding a black blueprint case . . ."

"Oh, God . . ." Sergejs is laughing so hard he can barely breathe, "and I thought girls only fall in love that stupidly in novels and sappy movies."

"You're the one who's dumb," Karolīna shoots back but without any real irritation. "But since I've gotten mixed up with you for a third time in my life, then I must really not be all that bright, that's a fact."

"This time it'll all be different," Sergejs isn't laughing anymore, but, tickling her lightly with his lips, whispering in her ear. "Obviously!" Karolīna says sarcastically and pulls the sleeping bag's hood over her head.

Karolīna wakes up perfectly rested, though it's too hot. The tent has been put up in a spot where the trees don't shield it from the morning sun, and gradually it transforms into a miniature sauna. Sergejs isn't in the tent, his empty sleeping bag lies next to her. Karolīna listens, but also doesn't hear anything outside other than the wind rustling the grass and tree leaves. She pulls down her sleeping bag's zipper, stretches well, and crawls out of the tent. She doesn't see Sergejs, but the ground in front of the tent is disturbed, the grass is strewn with open food packages, torn Rollton packs, bread crumbs. For a moment Karolīna stares in confusion at the chaos, then stands up and casts a gaze around the meadow and the closest bushes. He wouldn't have actually gone swimming in the sea by himself knowing there was no greater joy for Karolīna than soaking in the water. No, he didn't go, both towels are still hanging on the tree branch behind the tent, just where they left them yesterday.

Then she sees them . . . In the graveyard. In the maple tree. Feet clad in Sergejs's sneakers. Karolīna, feeling her way across the overgrown meadow grass in bare feet and not taking her eyes off of the gently swaying feet, she moves closer, leaves obscure the body and face, but those are unmistakably Sergejs's feet in those shoes, his legs in the camouflage pants with outer pockets on the sides, swaying stiffly, calmly, about a meter above the ground.

No, she won't go closer, she doesn't want to see it, she'll call the paramedics or lifeguards, Karolīna spins around and runs back to the tent, the phone is in her bag. No, first she needs to get Sergejs down, maybe everything isn't lost, but where is the knife? Where is the knife?! Karolīna digs around in the pockets of Sergejs's bag, last night he opened up the sausage packaging, she clearly saw a large, sharp pocket knife! Karolīna's hands are trembling, she's breathing heavily, desperately drawing air into her lungs, and can't order her movements or thoughts.

"What's up, sweetheart?" a voice says right by her ear.

"Augghhhh!" Karolīna shrieks louder than all of the living and dead members of the band Līvi combined, she shrieks loud enough to wake all the corpses—not just Sergejs—from their eternal rest.

"What are you looking for in my . . ." Sergejs asks sweetly, but isn't able to finish. Karolīna attacks him with his own bag and thrashes him across his head, his back, his hands, which he is using to protect his head.

"Monkey, idiot, don't you have any limits at all? Dumbass!"

She falls down onto her knees in the grass and starts sobbing loudly. Sergejs crouches down next to her and embraces her with both arms.

"Oh, come on . . . I was just pulling your leg, but look, you do love me. I'm important to you."

"Idiotic jokes! And how long were you hanging there waiting for me?" Karolīna is still shrieking.

"Actually, I was working out, there's a good branch for doing pull-ups . . . But then I saw you'd woken up and I thought I'd give you a little scare . . ."

"Little! A little scare!"

"Oh, shush, I'm sorry, I didn't know your nerves were so weak."

"Incorrigible is what you are . . . Incorrigible!"

Karolīna's hands are still shaking and after the yelling, her throat feels scratchy too. And she also feels her stomach contorting into spasms, which sometimes happens to her after major shocks, all that's missing is diarrhea, God help her.

The pain in her stomach eventually subsides, and Karolīna breathes a sigh of relief.

"Who was rampaging around here?" she finally asks looking around at the food and trash strewn about.

Sergejs sighs.

"I've got some bad news. We're out of food."

"You secretly ate it all overnight?"

"I left the bag of food hanging from a tree branch, I thought it would be too warm in the tent and it would start going bad . . . I heard the party overnight, yipping and yapping, but I never thought that the refreshments were ours. I didn't want to wake you by getting up, so I didn't even look. And now it is what it is . . . It's all gone. It looks like it was foxes . . ."

Karolīna doesn't say anything; now they need to find a path to the highway and go home. The weather is still wonderful, and her feet hurt much less than she had expected after trudging through the sand yesterday.

"What should we do?" she says after a silent moment.

"Should we go? I have two muesli bars in my bag, perfect for breakfast, and then we'll see. There might be a store in Jūrmalciems. I'm not really sure. We can walk out to the highway anytime, it's closer here than yesterday from Pape or Brušvīti.

Karolīna accepts the challenge, first they gather up the leftovers from last night's party and throw them away in the cemetery trash. Then they have breakfast and fill up their water bottles with the water they'd boiled and cooled last night. Sergejs had hung it up—kettle and all—in a different tree. One could say—with foresight—the water remained unruined by the foxes . . .

They walk back out to the beach again. The morning is hot and sunny, the sky a brilliant blue, only far out at sea is the horizon full of white, seemingly harmless, cumulus clouds.

"It looks like your feathery clouds were caught in a lie," Karolīna snickers.

"You're going to jinx it! They'll hear you and now will do everything they can to ruin the weather!" Sergejs mutters, and it seems funny to Karolīna that he actually sounds serious.

She shrugs and doesn't say anything else, and they both start walking north. According to the plan, today they have to walk eighteen kilometers, then tomorrow there'll be fifteen left. If they end up finding a store. The sea is choppier today, the wind sharper, but since it's so hot, the wind also feels pretty nice. Sergejs is scampering forward and back again, but Karolīna keeps her calm, measured gait and walks in the same direction the entire time. Seagulls, terns, and other birds that Karolīna doesn't know are flying overhead and gliding on the wind. It's good. Sergejs seems calmer today, not as keyed up as yesterday, and she likes that too. Maybe they'll stay together. Though trusting him would be the same as trusting the promises of politicians before elections. Sergejs has disappointed her twice. The first time when she was eighteen. The second time when she was forty. The first time she was completely infatuated with the young, rakish Don Juan, she lost her sense and innocence. The next time she believed him, he seemed grown up, more mature, perhaps somewhat tempered. He proposed, she accepted. And then he suddenly disappeared, a month later two promise-filled postcards from Slovenia dropped into her mailbox, one after the other. After a longer gap, there was one from Thailand, and then he vanished from Karolīna's life for fifteen years.

When Sergejs started writing her again on Facebook six months ago, Karolīna was single again. She could have taken a principled negative stance, but she still liked this crazy wanderer, and, if she was being completely honest, from time to time she had imagined him coming back, asking her forgiveness, swearing his love to her, and all kinds of other rose-colored dreams . . . And then they'd be happy and live till death do them part. It turned out that she still really liked Sergejs, but nothing else was left anymore. Not the butterflies in her stomach, not the sense of longing between their meetings. When she sees Sergejs's number flash on her phone, she sighs first, foreseeing an overly long conversation that finally tends toward the tedious, and only then answers the call: "Yes, sweetheart." An old, rusted out love. But now she was on a hike with Sergejs, to discover a new dimension to their relationship. Hilarious.

Sergejs has walked back toward her again.

"He's like a fart in a hot skillet, he can't sit still for a second," Karolīna thinks.

"Just past the dune there's a road parallel to the shore, it's less windy there," he says.

Karolīna is fine with moving behind the dune, the wind on the beach is tossing her hair in all directions and sometimes also throws a handful of sand in her face. Behind the dune it will be calmer. They climb up and keep walking along the grassy, well-driven road. It's hot, but they can walk here for a moment. If it gets too humid, then they'll go back out to the beach again. For a moment they walk alongside each other. A drop drips onto Karolīna's forehead. She looks up. The sky overhead is still clear and blue. Sergejs also knocks something off his cheek with the back of his hand. Now they're both looking up. Seagulls glide and swifts flash overhead.

"The birds must be sweating," Sergejs says solemnly.

Karolīna stares at him with wide eyes at first, and then falls into such a fit of laughter that she has to sit down on the roadside grass and laugh while her stomach twists into spasms again. Her laughter turns to groans, and Karolīna curls up and clutches her stomach.

"What's wrong? Your stomach hurts?"

"Uh huh . . ." Karolīna can only grunt.

"From what? Maybe your period is starting?"

"Oh, God, are you really that clueless? I went through menopause six years ago."

"How should I know . . . okay, but you have a first-aid kit. At least that's what we agreed?"

"The first-aid kit only has bandaging supplies. Iodine, gauze strips, antibacterial wipes, bandages. You didn't say to bring medication too. And anyway, my stomach spasms started in the morning when you hanged yourself. It's because of nerves, by the way," she adds pointedly.

"Fine, fine, just sit and wait, I'll go look around for something here."

He takes off his bag and puts it by Karolīna's feet, then darts off across the meadow. He zig-zags plucking something, sniffing it, rubbing it with this fingers, then throwing it on the ground and heading off to the next bunch. Karolīna's spasms come and go, she notices only now how many tiny, beautiful flowers are growing on the dunes. Most of them are low or creeping, yellow, blue, violet, rosy, only the wild rose bushes and baby's breath rise above them. They are blooming right now, in the sweltering heat they exude the aroma of a piss-filled jar of honey.

Sergejs darts over. He is holding a grayish-green stalk with catkins composed of tiny, yellow flowers.

"I found it!" he declares exuberantly. "Wormwood, a great remedy for stomach and intestinal problems. It should help."

"And how do you use it?"

"Wellll . . . I know that when the leaves are dry you pour boiling water over them and soak them for, I think, 20 minutes, we should look it up on Google. And then you drink it as a tea taking tiny sips every once in a while, it's supposed to be unbelievably bitter."

"Fine, dried leaves are used for tea. But these are fresh."

"The fresh ones should contain all the same ingredients as the dried ones, but not as concentrated. Maybe you should chew a leaf and not swallow it, just your saliva and the juice you chew out of it."

"Isn't wormwood what they use for making absinthe?"

"Well, yeah . . ." Sergejs admits fairly reluctantly. "But it only becomes hallucinogenic when combined with alcohol."

In the meantime, Karolīna has pulled her phone out from the depths of her bag and turned it on. Thank God, when she climbs up higher onto the dune, she gets a signal, and soon, twisting her face every so often because of the stomach pain, she finds information about wormwood.

"Caution! Wormwood is toxic!" Karolīna reads from the display. "A large dose can cause headache and vertigo. Overdosing can lead to uncontrollable diarrhea, unconsciousness, coma, and death . . . What are you trying to give me?"

"Uncontrollable diarrhea," Sergejs cackles.

"What are you laughing for, it also says coma and death! I'm not going to eat your wormwood, and the pain passed anyway, just like before, maybe it won't come back. We can keep going."

While bantering about the wormwood they both also rested a little from the hike. Karolīna turns off her phone and sticks it back into the bag, gets up, and notices only then that while Sergejs was running around the meadow and she was looking around on Google, the clouds had completely covered the sun. Overhead there are white, lumpy cumulus clouds, but Sergejs is looking out toward the sea, and Karolīna looks over too. A swath of dark blue stretches across the sea and seems to be moving right toward them.

"Let's pick up the pace a little, if it gets here, then that'll be in an hour or so, but by then maybe we will have gotten as far as Jūrmalciems," Sergejs says, this time sounding unusually serious and pragmatic.

They keep moving on. Karolīna tries to walk a little faster, but the movement doesn't match her inner pace, and soon enough she feels the resistance of her legs and hips, and so she returns to her usual speed.

"Maybe we should put up the tent and wait while it's raining? You said it was waterproof," Karolīna says to Sergejs who is ahead of her.

"And what do we do if it rains for a day and night straight? We also don't have any food left," he answers sensibly over his shoulder.

Sergejs is right and so they keep going. The clouds on the sea are coming faster than he had estimated, in half an hour, lightning and thunder are jolting the seaside air, and the wind is fiercely forcing the willows toward the ground and ruffling their clothing and hair. Out at sea, huge sheets of rain—black and sheer—can be seen descending from the clouds. Karolīna still thinks that they should pitch the tent. Sergejs has moved off ahead again and she tries to call out to him. The wind carries away her voice in the opposite direction.

Then big, piercing, but still only occasional, raindrops start falling. A moment later they stop, but it's clear that heavy rain is coming very soon and then there'll be no use trying to put up the tent. Karolīna shivers, thinking about sitting in a tent in completely soaked clothes when outside it's pouring rain. And if that diarrhea starts then, truly, the show's over . . . The feeling of helplessness practically makes her start crying.

Sergejs has climbed up to the top of the dune, turns around, and motions toward her, "Hey, walk faster, walk faster!" Karolīna can't go faster, she's tired and anxious, so she keeps on walking at her usual pace, but swings her arms at a wider angle. In the meantime, the rain has arrived, at first it's gentle, she can still take that, but then it starts coming harder and heavier. Karolīna, as much as she can, picks up the pace, but Sergejs has disappeared behind the dune. Karolīna can already feel raindrops on her scalp, her hair is soaked, and then Sergejs is running toward her over the dune without his bag or the tent, he runs up, takes her backpack, grabs her by the hand, and they both scramble forward, as fast as Karolīna's feet allow.

Just past the dune there is a canopy—four large posts and over them a slate roof. Who knows for what purpose it was built, maybe in the past sheep or some other farm animals sought shelter there during the rain, but right now it was a real gift for both of these seekers of new dimensions. Sergejs's bag and the tent are already sitting right in the center, and they both dart underneath the canopy at the same instant that a powerful crack of thunder and then rain loudly rattles the slate roof above their heads, and transforms into an opaque wall of water outside of the canopy.

"We made it," Sergejs says and hugs Karolīna. She exhales, expelling the air that she had drawn into her lungs while running and presses tightly against him.

"And what now?" Karolīna asks looking at the rivulet already running across the area protected by the canopy. Clearly it is on a slope, which is not really perceivable to the eye, but water, as always, finds the path of least resistance.

"Let's wait, if it doesn't pass, then we'll probably have to call someone. But I doubt we can get a signal down here . . ."

They stand for a moment embracing and not saying a word. Sergejs's arms are strong and warm. Outside it's thundering, flashing, and pouring, but right now they're safe here. The air is still muggy, they aren't cold. Right now, Karolīna feels like she could live with Sergejs. She could, but does she need to?

"Hello! What are you two doing here like a couple of little doves, planning to move in, or what?" a delicate, elderly voice suddenly says.

A tiny little lady with a brown, weathered face lined with dark creases is standing next to them under the canopy. Her pale blue eyes squint in a smile. The rain water streams off her long, green, rubberized poncho and hood and, without soaking into the sand, flows along the slope invisible to the eye.

"We're just here for a moment, sheltering from the rain," Sergejs explains apologetically.

"Well, if you like, you can stay here. I would gladly offer you some tea and a real roof over your heads, but I don't know if you'll like it in the house as much as out here."

Turning in her direction, they both notice that past the willows behind the canopy there is another slate roof. It's bigger, but when they were running through the rain, neither of them noticed it.

The house is small, old, and unrenovated, but inside it's pleasantly cozy. The kitchen is clean and bright, and the lady, once she's taken off her coat, turns out to be even smaller than she appeared at first.

"Anna," the lady says and extends a small hand hardened by work, but her handshake is rather energetic.

"Sergejs, and that's Karolīna," he answers for both of them.

"You managed to avoid it, aren't you completely soaked?"

"No," Karolīna says, and really only her hair is damp. Her clothes either didn't get wet or they dried on her body, she doesn't know. From all the excitement, her stomach twists into a new series of spasms, and this time she feels that she absolutely has to go.

"I'm sorry," she says blushing. "Can I use your bathroom?"

"Oh, honey, you'll have to go outside. I don't have fancy facilities like in the city. Here's an umbrella."

She takes it off a nail, which is right on the inside of the door.

"Come, I'll show you where the outhouse is."

Anna takes her outside and shows her the path leading around the corner of the house and, Karolīna, opening her umbrella, takes off in that direction. She gets there at the last second and then has some time to examine and admire the tidy outhouse and, as would be expected, the heart-shaped opening in the door. A cloth bag containing toilet paper rolls is nailed onto the wall and embroidered with text saying: "What you leave here is a gift from the Lord, go forth grateful and reassured." Karolīna is profoundly touched and really does feel grateful . . .

The rain is still coming down in buckets and while walking back, Karolīna notices a familiar name on the corner of the building. The name of the house is "Klaušnieki"! She cheerfully heads inside and wants to tell Sergejs that maybe they've happened upon a relative of his or at least a home belonging to his family, but, stepping across the threshold, she suddenly feels confused. Three little faces, three pixies with black, curly hair are sitting together with Anna and Sergejs at the table, each with a steaming bowl of soup before them, and there's an extra place set, that one must be for her.

"Come on in, here is a bowl where you can wash your hands, and I already poured you some soup. These are my great-granddaughters, my granddaughter Elīna and her husband Saul are visiting this week, they live somewhere in England, I can't remember the city, but this morning they drove to Liepāja, to the Anna's Day Market, so I have to look after Amy, Rosie, and Natalie—she calls out the girls' names with practiced care, it's clear that learning them took a certain degree of effort.

The tiny dark faces smile upon hearing their names, their white teeth glint, each girl is smaller than the next, they might be from five to eight years old. Karolīna doesn't dare ask if they speak Latvian. And so they all sit and eat this heavenly vegetable soup made with baby carrots and green peas straight from the garden. The girls also eat with abandon, instead of rejecting it, as can often be the case with children these days.

"I'll be right back," Anna is first to finish her small bowl and heads out of the kitchen through the other door.

"We should call someone to come pick us up," Karolīna says.

"Anna said it's not far to the bus stop, maybe a kilometer to the Liepāja-Klaipēda highway and then three hundred more meters in the direction of Liepāja. Well, that's if we can't reach anyone by phone."

Amy, Rosie, and Natalie move their heads as they follow their conversation. As soon as Karolīna and Sergejs stop talking, the three girls grab their spoons and continue eating.

Then the door opens, and Anna comes in. She's holding a rather large bamboo plate, on which rosy and yellow apples and green pears are arranged in concentric circles, on top of them are blue plums, everything is decorated with dill and marigold blossoms. A stumpy candle is burning right in the middle, and Anna—her cheeks flushed—starts her speech:

"Karolīna, while you were outside, Sergejs explained your bad luck and how the plans he had for celebrating your birthday were all ruined, and so I decided to cheer you up—even if just a little."

It's not Karolīna's birthday, Karolīna was born in November, she opens her mouth to object, but Anna starts singing the Latvian birthday song, "Daudz baltu . . ." in a delicate, trembling voice. Sergejs, holding back his laughter, tries to sing along, but their voices get lost. The little pixies jump to their feet and—in a wonderful choral trio devoid of any tonality, but imbued with childlike clarity, each with her individual melody but with the same rhythm—sing brightly:

"Happy birthday to you, happy birthday to you, happy birthday, dear aunty, happy birthday to you!"

And they repeat the song three times, until Karolīna comes around and blows out the burning candle . . . Amy, Rosie, and Natalie applaud. "Thank you, Anna, you're so very kind," she says from the bottom of her heart.

"Dear, you're welcome to whatever I've grown here . . ." Karolīna takes one of the rosy apples and takes a bite out of it, it's juicy and sweet, just like the fruit from the tree of knowledge in paradise.

"Anna, can I ask you about your house?"

"Why not?" Anna answers with interest.

"Outside I saw that your house is called "Klaušnieki," and in the cemetery nearby we saw Sergejs and Karolīna Klaušnieks. Do you have any connection with them?" she wants to continue and say that Sergejs is the grandson of this Klaušnieks couple, but just at that moment Sergejs has a coughing fit—is he choking on the plum that he took from Karolīna's "birthday" present? Karolīna slaps Sergejs on the back until his cough gradually relents.

In the meantime, Amy, Rosie, and Natalie have emptied their soup bowls and are watching everything unfold with wide eyes. Anna points to the bowls and asks in Latvian: "grib vēl?"—do you want more? Then looks at the next one and asks again: "grib vēl?" All three of them shake their heads and smile. Anna gathers the plates and opens the door to the adjacent room, pointing to show them that they have to go there now. The girls are obedient and head out, the little one goes last, and she turns toward Sergejs and Karolīna, waves with her little hand, and squeaks:

"Bye-bye!"

Now Anna can answer.

"I do, I do, dear, a very direct connection."

Karolīna looks happily over at Sergejs, he is sitting stiffly and staring at the table.

"Karolīna and Sergejs were my stepparents. Sergejs had a different last name, something like Bedņaga or Bedolaga, and when he married Karolīna, he took her last name, so it wouldn't sound so dreary. She was a Klaušnieks. Right after the wedding, Sergejs was drafted, it was the first war, in 1914, not the Great Patriotic War. He came back practically unscathed, except for a shot that

200

hit him in the groin, and so he couldn't have children of his own. My parents, on the other hand, had eight. At first I worked as a herder for the Klaušniekses, but then they asked my mom if I could stay here to help them, they promised to take good care of me. I'm not adopted, but even so I've lived here since I was nine, during the Russian years, the German years, every year. They left the house to me in their will. They were really good people, really good . . . Oh, but you're also Sergejs and Karolīna, just like my dear ones, I didn't even notice at first.

Anna's eyes fill with tears.

Karolīna feels how anger has made her face flushed. Sergejs had lied to her again. Gramps and Granny, of course! But just then Sergejs gets up, pulls a small box out of his pocket, drops to one knee and says:

"Karolīna, on this strange day that I had planned to be completely different, but which has in the end turned out to be so strange and beautiful, may I ask for your hand?"

Karolīna, honestly, no longer understands if this is a comedy or a tragedy, or simply grotesque, she doesn't want to laugh, but howl loudly—though with an enthusiasm bordering on hysteria, she exclaims:

"Yes, yes, my love! Yes!"

He opens the box and takes out a ring, Karolīna has no relevant experience and so she can't tell how expensive or fancy it is, thank God, the ring fits, and in the meantime Sergejs has already successfully put it on her ring finger.

Anna is wiping away tears.

"How beautiful, how beautiful, and when you're not so young anymore, that is so . . ." she mutters quietly to herself, lifts the kettle off the stove top with the heated water, and turns her back to them to wash the dishes.

"Anna, the rain has stopped, thank you so much for your hospitality. We'll probably be on our way to the bus stop," Karolīna says as she glares at Sergejs.

Anna shakes off her wet hands, wipes them on the towel over her shoulder, and turns toward them. Her warm smile fills every tiniest wrinkle of her face, she is so happy about all the beautiful things that just took place before her eyes.

"I'd promised you tea but look, I completely forgot."

"Unless you have wormwood," Sergejs says, "then we'll stay a moment longer, Karolīna definitely could use it."

"No, no, thank you," Karolīna objects, "maybe you know what time that bus might come?"

"If you leave right now, then it will be right there. It's fifteen minutes to the stop, maybe a bit more, but the bus should come in half an hour."

"Then we'll head out, thank you so much."

"I'll put those birthday apples in a bag, then you'll have something to snack on, maybe you'll take a few all the way home too . . ."

"Thank you, Anna," Karolīna says again with genuine warmth.

"All the best, only the best, harmony hand in hand until your last day," Anna extends her delicate hand to say farewell and squeezes theirs tightly, then strokes Karolīna's hand. "All the best, the very best."

*

Karolīna and Sergejs are walking in step, both next to each other. They walk without talking. They walk for a long time, the highway visible at the end of the gravel road. Sergejs is the first to break.

"Karolīna, I was just kidding about my grandparents. It wasn't without reason, you weren't ready to spend the night there, otherwise we would've needed to keep going, and who knows where we'd find water. And imagine the luck—to find a Karolīna and Sergejs!"

Sergejs is right. If it hadn't been for the story about the grandparents, Karolīna would have kept arguing for much longer about where they'd spend the night. Maybe she would have even left on her own. She's still unbelievably angry.

"And why did you need to say something to Anna about a birthday?"

"Well . . . We had to talk about something, and I . . ."

"You're a pathological liar."

"I was just kidding!"

"Me too!"

"What do you mean, me too?" Sergejs asks suspiciously.

"I was joking too! Take it!"

She slips the ring off her finger and presses it into his palm.

"You didn't think that I would really stick my head in a noose of my own free will?"

Disappointment washes across Sergejs's face but disappears in an instant. He weighs the ring in his palm for a moment, then pulls the box out of his pocket, and carefully pushes the ring into the velvet holder. Then he sticks the box back into his pocket."

"Well, fine. Don't leave yet. You can still think about it. Let's go."

He heads toward the bus stop in his bounding, youthful gait with his gray bag and the tent on his back.

Karolīna pulls another rosy apple out of the bag and, as she chews on it, gradually falls back from Sergejs.

She goes at her own pace. Calmly and effortlessly.

THE WHITE HOUSE AT THE TOP OF THE HILL

I'm sorry.

I don't know if you need to hear that, but even if you won't answer, it's important for me to say it. I'm sorry.

I'm having a small party Saturday. I'd be so happy to see you there. In the afternoon. At the white house. You know, I'm still living in the white house.

Lilija has just poured the hot water for her morning coffee. She drops one whole teaspoon of grounds into the large, dark green cup adorned with angular designs, which looks Indian, but it's hard to say whether from the sub-continent or North America. A little bit of cinnamon with bergamot, some vanilla, and plenty of steamed milk. White, light, aromatic coffee without sugar. Clutching the cup with both hands in her usual way—as if it didn't also have a large, comfortable handle—Lilija warms her freezing fingers. They always feel freezing. She studies her short-clipped nails, cracked hangnails, and the dry, pale, wrinkled skin of the top of her hand. She makes a fist and releases it, watching the veins wriggling underneath like blue worms. When her fingers feel warm enough, Lilija puts down her cup and looks out the window. For years her morning ritual has never changed. Coffee. Fingers. Window. But now there was that letter. It had ruined the rhythm. It was wriggling around like a worm, but much deeper and less predictable than the veins plainly visible underneath the shiny, creased skin of her hands.

An open envelope with no stamp or address. Delicate lowercase letters, all of about the same size, and ornate uppercase letters with calligraphic flourishes. Lilija gazes at the note for a moment, she studies every line, every curve and loop, she has seen this handwriting before. But she can not recall who has written it . . . There are so many things she can no longer remember.

The phone rings, Lilija realizes she was so engrossed in the letter that she hadn't even finished her coffee. Her daughter always calls twice a day at exactly the same time—at nine in the morning, and at six in the evening. Lilija moves swiftly, taking tiny steps to reach the phone. It is still in the exact same spot on the shelf in the front hall it's been for the last decades.

"Good morning, Mom!"

"Good morning, Mar . . . Žan . . . Ingrīda," Lilija is unsure as she responds.

"Žanete, Mom, it's me—Žanete."

"Yes, Žanete, I know, I'm sorry."

"How did you sleep? How do you feel? I'll stop by tonight. Do you need anything?"

Behind three houses on the tiny side street there is a little shop. In a pinch you can buy what you need there or get it on credit. Luīze, the small, chubby shopkeeper, has tiny hands and thin fingers. She is up early in the morning kneading dough, whisking eggs, and baking pastries, all the while sneezing and laughing. "I'm allergic to wheat flour," she happily announces to anyone who turns up at the moment she sneezes four or five times in a row like a cat. On Mondays she conjures up all kinds of wonderful flaky pastries—croissants, napoleons, elephant ears, and cheese straws. On Wednesdays, it's apple cake made with yeast dough, and sinfully indulgent cheesecake, cinnamon coffee cake, mushroom and bacon pasties, but on Fridays, it's cream puffs, cupcakes with fruit and caramel cream, éclairs, and other fancy things. "You can't have everything at once or available every day, otherwise customers get used to it and stop appreciating it," Luīze says. "But if they're forced to wait a week, then they know its value. They'll stop by the night before, give me a wink, and add their names to the list. I have to make sure that I bake enough for everybody. They've spent that time anticipating it. And anticipation can make even a pastry more valuable, desirable." Arnolds, the owner, is often behind the counter. A slim, raven-haired fifty-year-old with a humped nose, brown eyes that seem permanently startled, and constantly trembling nostrils, just like those of a spooked Arabian horse. "Every smell and stench in the store muse his mucous membranes, that can't be easy," thinks Lilija. She knows that her own nose with its delicate and nuanced sense of smell has been her enemy her entire life.

"I don't think I need anything," Lilija hesitates before answering her daughter. There's still enough coffee, she remembers that. "Žanete? What day is it today?"

"Saturday," Žanete says curtly, "Why do you ask?"

"That's what I thought, Luīze baked éclairs yesterday, and so, yes, then yesterday was Friday and today is Saturday," Lilija concludes quite logically without answering why she needed to know what day it was.

"OK, Mom, then I'll be by sometime after five."

Lilija shoots a sideways glance at the letter on the table. Saturday. In the afternoon, at the white house. Today is Saturday, Žanete had said. Lilija couldn't really remember the way to the white house, it's been so long. Lately she only goes as far as Luīze and Arnolds's store by herself on Wednesdays and Fridays. She doesn't like Monday's flaky pastries, they're too crumbly and dry. She definitely remembers, though, that she has to climb up to the house, that it's high up, that there is a wide street that runs right along in front of it, but to reach it, she has to scale a narrow path paved with cobblestones. Lilija is sure that once she goes outside, her steps will lead her to the white house.

She gets dressed and selects clothes that feel light and easy on her body. Her faded linen skirt with ruffles and white embroidered cotton blouse match the blooming white lilacs out front. When she walks onto the street, Lilija rests for a moment on her cane and looks in one direction and then the other several times. The path leading past the lilacs leads to the pastry shop. Lilija has the feeling that the correct way is in the other direction. She turns and slowly, but with an air of certainty, heads down the narrow sidewalk, which hugs the edge of the wide, asphalt street.

"It was definitely a good idea to bring the cane," she concludes after just a few blocks. Lilija hardly ever uses it when she walks to Luīze and Arnolds's little shop, only on days when a magnetic storm is raging, which has a profound effect on her sense of well-being, disturbs her blood pressure, and can make her extremely dizzy. But today is a good day. Walking down the sloping street, her cane is just the right companion. And she'll still need to climb back up later. Lilija realizes that she must have left the letter back at home on the table . . . "Eh," she grouses, "well, what can you do," she opens up her knit purse and rummages around for a moment examining her wallet, comb, mirror, lipstick, two old theater programs—oh God, it had been so long since Lilija had been to the theater!—then also a few old receipts, a card with a picture of the Virgin Mary. No, Lilija isn't all that sure of her beliefs, she's probably not a believer, but sometimes she gets a little scared, what if God does exist after all, and what will happen at the appointed hour when she'll have to stand before Him and answer for all of her sins and mistakes, for the answered prayers that caused nothing but pain and disappointment. Lilija wants to truly believe, but belief isn't something you can plant in someone's head like a seed in the ground. Believe or don't believe, and if you doubt your own belief, then it's clear you don't really believe.

The letter isn't in her purse. Just a hint of lavender. Lilija always makes sure everything around her smells clean and fresh and not, heaven forbid, stagnant or stinking.

*

"You smell good," He always said when He'd hug Lilija. She never believed Him and was always consumed by doubt because the constant movement, work, and heat caused her to sweat; I stink like a horse—that was her first thought in the middle of the day when He suddenly burst through the door, like a swift wind, unexpected and yet so welcome. "Wait, I'm sweaty, I'll wash off," she awkwardly wriggled out of His embrace. "No, no, stop." He took a deep breath, His nose pressed against Lilija's short, trim, but still lush, black hair. "You smell like a woman, like a real woman, do you understand?" Lilija blushed and didn't believe Him. "How long are you going to stay?" "Two months, maybe a little more," He said unconvincingly, turning away as if something in the room had changed, was new. Nothing ever changed in Lilija's home, except perhaps the tablecloth, the rug by the bed, a new cup replacing a broken one, a different indoor plant, a candle taking the place of one that had burned down, a new photograph behind the glass in the cabinet. Nothing changed. Except for her as she slowly aged, twenty-six, thirty, thirty-three . . .

After a week He would always grow quiet. Every night His arms would still wrap tightly around her body. Lilija could never stop being amazed by how perfectly they fit together, it was as if her ample flesh was meant for His lean, defined bones, which she could almost count. And sometimes Lilija would do exactly that: a collarbone, shoulders, one, two, three ribs, a masculine, solid nipple (brushed by her lips), four, five, stop, that tickles, a narrow pelvis, a hip bone, skin, lips, breath, tongue. He didn't count Lilija's bones, and it wasn't even so easy to do, His hands and lips trailed across her warm, tense flesh over and over again, she'd lost count how many times. Then, holding her close, still burning with heat, He would inhale deeply from the space between her breasts, pulling the air into His nostrils. "What do I smell like," she asked. "At night, like freshly baked bread, in the morning, a little bitter, like marigolds or sometimes like green apples, and then you also have a smell that I can't describe, maybe that's the real one, the one that's just yours," He laughed. "That one is rare though, only there when I'm about to leave." He fell silent. "I love you, do you know that?" "Yes. I know," she answered, smelling like warm bread.

At the end of the second week, His embrace hadn't loosened. In truth, it never did. But sometimes at night He would jolt upright with a gasp, which sounded a bit like a cry. Lilija knew that soon He would stop talking. Then He would become irritable. And then one morning after another week, He would pull her so close that she wouldn't even be able to see into His eyes, He would bury His lips in her thick hair, and every one of His words would feel like warm, heavy stone against her scalp as He spoke them—"I just can't anymore, I need to go. I'll come back."

Lilija had walked part way down the hill. She hadn't turned down any of the small side streets—their yards bubbling over with blushing bursts of burnet roses and clouds of blooming lilacs in every color under the sky, their air filled with the pungency of the nearby shore, the fleeting scent of flowers, and the always present odor of cat and human urine. The street levels out here and Lilija stops for a moment. It's cool, the sun drenches the city with light and heat, but even so Lilija always feels a bit cold. She stands there with her hand lifted to shade her eyes and looks first in one direction, then the other. A few flushed passersby in summery clothes, necks dotted with sweat, and skin blushing in the light of the first sunny day, walk past her quietly, as if they were moving through her, all going in the same direction, but Lilija doesn't know, nor does she even sense that her path heads in the opposite direction. Every few moments, a gust of hot wind blows her linen skirt and hair about. Her hair is still thick and strong, but now completely gray. She continues on her way at an unhurried pace, supporting herself on her cane. In a flash she feels she remembers the way and that on the next side street she needs to turn right. With the sun staring at her back, her black shadow sliding in front of her, Lilija's white form is right on its heels.

Back then, Lilija's apartment had no running water. Every day she had to walk to the water pump two blocks away with a bucket in one hand and a smaller jug in the other—she didn't need as much water for drinking. She used the water sparingly. Her arms were so weak and it was so heavy to carry. When He would suddenly show up again, He would bring her so much that she was able to soak and splash in it to her heart's content. He would usually fill the large kettles on the wood stove in the kitchen with water, light the fire, and then place the tin washtub already filled with cool water right next to it on the floor. "I got you your water," He'd say, "wash, swim, dive into it like a mermaid, soothe away all your worries. And think of me while you're washing. I'm going for a walk, I need to cool down. And I'll be thinking about you, all the time about you. You know I love you, don't you? And then I'll be back."

The door would slam shut and Lilija would pour some of the hot water from the kettles into the cool tub with a smile, washing, diving into like a mermaid, and soothing away her worries. And she would think of Him. She would utter a silent prayer for something to change, for something to happen that would make Him stay and never leave again. Maybe not this time, maybe next time or after three more times. It slowly grew dark outside. There was plenty of water in the tub and it had been heated on an open flame, Lilija was beaming, warm all the way through, and felt truly alive.

He came home then with damp hair, excited and playful as a puppy. "Leave the lights off," He whispered in Lilija's ear, lifting her warm and soft body with His cool arms, to carry her into the bedroom. They caressed each other slowly, Lilija ran her fingertips across the scales covering His body, so that's why He didn't want the lights on, He's turned into a scaly sea monster; Lilija could smell the sea in His hair and taste the salt on His scaly skin. "Where were you, what happened to you," she laughed, when they stopped they both were holding each other tightly again, mirroring each other's form with their bodies. "Lilija, I found a house! I'll buy you a house, have you seen it—there, on the west side of the city, at the very highest point. Built from white stones with a red tin roof. The white house at the top of the hill, I'll buy it for you." Lilija kept laughing, tracing shapes with her fingers on His scaly back. "Don't laugh, please, I'm going to make a lot of money and buy you that house."

"Why is your skin covered with scales? I thought you'd turned into a fairytale dragon and were going to spirit me away to who knows where. I thought you'd take me with you and we'd stay together. Every day, every moment. You want to stay together, don't you?" He laughed, leapt out of bed, and turned on the light. "I went swimming in the sea, I didn't have a towel, but I ran back so quickly to be with you that the wind dried all the sand and seaweed onto my body. Yes, I'm a sea monster now." Lilija looked with wide eyes at His skin, the sheets, the floor, there was white sand and dried seaweed everywhere. I'm sorry, He said, "I'm going to rinse off in the water you were soaking in while you waited for me. And then I'll clean everything up." Lilija laughed, and her tears fell down onto the sandy sheets.

The walk has made her a little tired, but here was the small park with the fountain, she remembers it, nothing has changed. Lilija sits down on the bench next to two stone fish, which are vomiting water straight into the air, they're tightly entwined, just like she had once been with someone else, Lilija tenses as she tries to remember that person's name, but it's gone, mixed in with the rest of that pile of people, places, and events. She can't arrange them properly in her mind or recall the special place she had put any of them so as not to forget them later. He has no name, Lilija relaxes, she has never had any luck when she has let herself grow anxious and tried to force something. Instead, when she needs to remember something she has forgotten, it will usually spring up at the least expected moment. Lilija looks at the wet, awkward bodies and thick lips of the fish. Clouds have covered the sky, and though the world still appears bright, gusts of wind are chasing each other through the tops of the linden trees, shaking them. There's a sound like threatening whispers, and then everything is calm again. Lilija has no sense of how much time has passed since she started on her way. She is a little tired, it is still cool, but it feels like her destination should soon arrive. After the park she still has to walk past the small, fuchsia-colored Orthodox church, then turn right again, and then, yes, then there should be a cobbled path leading up. And at the very top of the hill—the white house where she can finally find peace. Lilija knows she is expected there.

And then Lilija got her wish, He stayed. After three or five more times, He couldn't leave anymore. Lilija had noticed during the last few times how His breathing, which had always been quiet, was now rattling and wheezing instead. He no longer burst in like the wind, He didn't carry Lilija in His arms anymore. Every time He entered her house it was like its entire volume, its full depth and height, were filled by Him. From the ceiling down to even the tiniest corner, everything became part of Him—fresh, serene, strong, and resonant. Lilija would dive into Him, swim in Him, flowing into His clarity, absorbing His freshness, and deeply breathing in His strength. And then, imperceptibly, it all slowly began to fade. The space was still filled by Him, but it felt different, maybe even a little heavy . . . "You know I love you, don't you," He held her hands as if He were pleading with her, afterward He would hold her in an insecure, but still warm embrace. "You smell nice," a tired voice wheezed into the hair near her ear." "What do I smell like," Lilija asked. "I'll stay here, my love, with you. Forever," He said, without answering her question. Lilija wanted to feel happy, but she didn't. "My prayers have been answered, finally, He will stay here," she repeated to herself flatly over and over again.

*

Lilija continues walking slowly, she exits the park and looks around with confusion. Everything here is not as she remembers. There's no chapel and the streets run in completely different directions, not in the direction she needs to turn to reach the white house. While Lilija is standing there befuddled, occasional, heavy drops start falling from the sky, they hit her skin here and there and leave gray, transparent, wet spots on her white clothing. It's cold. Lilija steps to one side of the sidewalk and stands underneath a large maple tree. Its trunk is scarred and warm, Lilija presses up tightly against it; the rain is starting to fall harder and heavier, but she feels safe here.

Several young people run past her laughing and shrieking without noticing the woman stranded under the tree. A man in a suit with an umbrella rushes by quickly. Lilija looks on, gripping her cane tightly, she is confused, tired, and now rather cold. A group of boys approaches her, they're confident, calm, the rain falls over their dark faces and black eyes, but they don't run or try to avoid it. As they come closer, Lilija hears them speaking in a strange language filled with nasal, guttural sounds. Their sentences begin somewhere above their heads and then fall whistling and jostling to the earth along with the rain, sinking into the puddles already collecting in the cracks in the asphalt.

"Puis-je vous aider, madame?"

Lilija grows frightened and at the same moment catches sight of his dark face and brown eyes. He smells like seaweed and in an instant he has filled Lilija's entire world with a strange, pungent, but somehow pleasant odor. Lilija stares at his face, a little stream of rain flows slowly from his temple down past his chin, and she holds her purse closer to her breast.

"Puis-je vous aider?" he says again, Lilija doesn't understand a word and only shakes her head. No, no, she won't go along with the boy, she won't give him her purse, she won't give up, she'll scream if she has to. And just in case she grips her cane even more tightly.

The other boys say something in the strange language and the leader apparently changes his mind. He smiles at Lilija and returns to his friends. They walk away, the boy turns around one more time and looks at her, but doesn't return, the acrid odor lingers everywhere around her, Lilija, shaking from fear and cold, breathes it in deeply several times. It irritates her nose and makes her feel drowsy.

The downpour stops. The maple tree protected Lilija fairly well, a bit of moisture has soaked into her clothes and hair, but she really did avoid getting drenched. The sun peeks out from behind the clouds and in an instant everything around her is aglitter. Lilija remains under the maple for just a moment longer, but the strange, drowsy smell had dissipated, and, leaning heavily against her cane, she walks out into the light.

He really tried. But Lilija didn't know how to be with Him when He was like this. The rooms were still filled by Him, but there was no freshness or clarity. And now it was all the time, every day, every hour, every moment. The air grew stagnant, thick, hard to breathe . . . She was slowly drowning. He was growing weaker every day, the packaging and bottles for His pills were piling up, the doctors only shook their heads. He asked for forgiveness. "I love you, I'm sorry, you know I love you." She brought water for them both and every moment she could, she ran to the sea. To go for a swim, stand naked in the wind, breathe in, to feel strong and free. And to fight and battle the thoughts reminding her how she had hoped for this, prayed for it. Let Him stay here with her. Let it come to pass that He stays.

A year and a half later He had a heart transplant. "It's a miracle," He said, when after the surgery they were permitted to exchange a few words for the first time. "A miracle." Lilija stood at His bedside dressed in a sterile hospital gown with a mask on her face and wept. He recovered, His doctors nodded approvingly at every appointment. Everything went according to plan and two months after the operation He returned home.

"I've lost my sense of smell," He said quietly as He came into the room. "I can't smell a thing anymore." Lilija was afraid to embrace Him, so fragile, even more gaunt and transparent than before, and with a stranger's heart beating in His chest. She kept bringing water for them both, a month later He joined her and carried the jug of drinking water, and it wasn't too much longer before He would start bringing all the water again for their shared home.

His sense of smell didn't return. And they slept without touching at night. On weekends they would go on walks, exchanging words and phrases that were so unimportant that later on neither of them could even remember what they had talked about. Only once when a man walked toward them with a dog, a brown, wiry, and frisky dachshund, He grabbed Lilija's hand without even realizing it. "Hello, Mr Engelmanis." "Hello, how are you doing, how do you feel," answered the slender, very tall man, deftly removing his glasses. "I'm really doing quite well," He answered calmly. "Everything is good and I'll be seeing you again soon. For a check-up." "I'm happy you're following my advice to walk, move, live a full life," the doctor said leaning down a bit in a tone that left no room for disagreement. His white teeth flashed below his dark glasses. The dachshund was fidgeting and had wrapped its leash around the doctor's legs—it yelped impatiently. "Have a good day, Mr Engelmanis. Thank you."

He let go of her hand immediately. They walked in silence for a moment. "I didn't ask them what they did with my heart. During that entire time, I didn't ask about it even once, not before, not after." Lilija didn't know what to say. "They have rules after all, instructions, I don't know, utilization procedures. You could still ask about it." He was quiet for another moment. "I wouldn't believe them," He finally said forcing the words across His lips. "I don't know where my heart is."

At night He tossed and moaned. Lilija stretched out her hand and put it soothingly on His shoulder, but it didn't help. Lilija slid out of the warm bed without turning on the light and went into the kitchen. She dipped a cup into the half-empty jug, took a few sips, and poured the rest back. Back in the room He was sitting up in bed staring at the wall. "Lilija, I had a dream." Lilija crawled back into her place, the sheet and blanket gently nestled her in the warmth she had stored and saved up herself. "I had a dream," He said again. But Lilija didn't say anything, and

He kept speaking quietly. "I woke up during the operation but I couldn't speak or move. I saw everything. Engelmanis tossed my heart into an aluminum tray and everyone pretended not to see anything. The nurses, anesthesiologist, assistants. There was a crowd of people there and no one gave a single thought to Engelmanis throwing my heart into a tray under the operating table." He was quiet for a moment. Then continued. "And then he finished sewing up my chest and walked out, I stayed on the table naked and empty, completely powerless, until I suddenly felt I could get up, I could stand, and I decided to follow Engelmanis. I shouldn't have looked back, but I did and saw myself lying on the operating table, naked, empty, with a dark red seam down the middle of my chest, restrained by cables, a tube coming out of my mouth. I hesitated for a moment, but then left myself lying there and went with Engelmanis."

Lilija was getting cold. She wrapped her blanket tighter around herself and pulled her knees up to her chest.

"We went to the doctor's house. He was casually carrying the tray in his hand, I thought I could hear an occasional heartbeat echoing deeply against its aluminum sides. I think he knew I was there with him. Because when we got to his house, he unlocked the door and slipped inside so quickly that I wasn't able to dash in with him and so had to stay outside. I stood there for a moment not sure what to do next, I'm not sure for how long. Time passes at a different rate in dreams than in real life."

He grew quiet again. Then He turned His head toward Lilija, in the darkness the space where His eyes would be appeared only as two black hollows. "And then I smelled it." He continued.

"You know I've lost my sense of smell . . . But I clearly smelled the odor of cooked meat with onions, bay leaves, spices, and a little bit of garlic. I snuck up to the window, the light was on inside, there were no curtains, and Engelmanis was using a knife to slice small pieces off my heart. Off a grayish-brown, steaming heart fresh out of the pot. He was cutting it into pieces, but on the ground was the dachshund, standing up on its hind legs, whirling around him. The doctor let out a cheery laugh and every now and again would say—speak! And as soon as the dachshund barked, he would drop a piece of my heart into its mouth."

Lilija couldn't stand to listen to any more, she wrapped her head in the blanket and laid down on her stomach. He stopped talking. He sat for a moment, and then also laid down and stared at the ceiling. That's how they remained until the morning. Maybe one of them dozed off for a moment, maybe not. The next morning, Lilija woke up first and made Him breakfast.

When He walked into the kitchen, Lilija went to Him and hugged Him. His body shuddered with involuntary resistance. Lilija pressed her head close to Him so that her short, thick hair scattered across His face, and was quiet for a moment. "What do I smell like? What does my hair smell like?" His body kept resisting. "You know that I can't smell anything," He muttered. "Do you love me?" Lilija asked in a more demanding tone, lifting her gaze and staring right into His eyes.

"I don't know," He turned away. "I don't know," He said a little louder. "I don't know if it's even possible to love with this strange heart. I don't know," He was almost screaming. His body was strong again, and His breath didn't wheeze or rattle, but He had lost His sense of smell. Completely.

"Then leave!" Lilija screamed back at Him. "I can't and don't want this anymore. I have no strength, every room is filled with you, there's nothing else, you're everywhere, in every space, from the walls to the ceiling, it's just you, so heavy and impenetrable. There's no room for me here anymore, I'm slowly disappearing, drowning, dissolving into you and into hopelessness. Go away! You don't need me anymore, you're strong, much stronger than before."

Leaving the shelter of the maple tree, Lilija suddenly sees the small, fuchsia-colored chapel exactly where it had always been. Where earlier, before the rain, she couldn't find it. Smiling to herself and a bit cross about her earlier agitation, Lilija turns wearily in its direction and is now rather certain that it's only a short distance to the white house. The air is brilliantly clear and refreshing, the aroma of fresh grass, lilacs, and wet asphalt is coming from all directions.

Lilija walks slowly, supporting herself on her cane, the road leads upward at a steady angle, but she knows that the final stretch will be the most difficult. Still, Lilija is ready to walk, climb up, climb into herself, right now the white house seems like the endpoint of a long, difficult pilgrimage where she will at long last find peace and absolution . . . She passes the church, turns right, and after a few dozen meters more of a steady climb, she finally catches sight of the white house shining in the sun at the end of the steep, cobbled side street. Lilija feels simultaneously relieved and anxious. Only this climb remains, it's steeper than it is long. Catching her breath, she clutches her cane and heads up. It would be easier if the sun wasn't in her eyes. "If I can't manage all of it at once, I'll rest halfway," Lilija consoles herself. And slowly, thoughtfully, and with the support of her trusty cane, she reaches her destination. Lilija stands in front of the house, looking at its white stone walls, then tips her head back and looks at the red tin roof glittering in the sunlight. Finally, she lifts her shaking hand and, her heart in somersaults, rings the doorbell.

A young woman opens the door, she looks so much like Him that Lilija is confused for a second. For a moment, the young woman looks at Lilija like she's seen a miracle, then jumps across the threshold and hugs her. The woman smells like the sea, just like He did, but also in some other way that seems familiar to Lilija, but she can't quite place it.

"My God, where were you all this time, I had no idea what to think or do, I'd run over to Luīze and Arnolds's, but they said that they hadn't seen you since yesterday, you upset them too. They said to call if I needed help looking for you. I almost called the police, Mom, where were you? Where were you walking, Mom, and what's with that letter on the kitchen table, who did you write it to?"

Lilija slowly steps across the threshold and walks into her house. Her fatigue prevents her from speaking, she walks to the guest room and falls into the large, soft chair. On the way, Žanete pops into the kitchen, grabs the letter off the table, pours some water from the carafe into a glass, then comes into the room, covers Lilija's knees with a quilt, hands her the water, and, sitting on the floor next to Lilija's chair, nestles up close to her legs.

"Who were you writing it to?"

223

Lilija greedily drinks the water, then stops—her memory suddenly snaps into place and spits out the name that Lilija had been trying to remember for so long.

"To Karels."

"Karels, Mom? Dad died," Žanete stares into Lilija's eyes as she speaks. "Dad died twenty-five years ago. Don't you remember?"

Lilija puts the glass down and pulls the quilt up higher. She really is cold.

"Mom, I'll move back in with you, okay? It'll be easier for me, I won't have to pay rent, and there's more room here. We can take care of things, it'll be cheaper for both of us, I'll help you do everything around the house, what do you think?"

"You already help," Lilija says as if she had just woken up. "But what about your job? It'll be such a long trip for you."

"It'll be okay, I'll manage. So, is that a yes? I'll stay in my room." Žanete is smiling, but her eyes are clouded over and dark.

They were already living in the white house when Žanete was born. The scar from Lilija's Caesarean section was healing just as fully and completely as Karels's opened chest had once.

When Karels leaned over His wife at night and lay on top of her with His lean, sinuous frame, to caress each of her most secret and sensitive spots with His mouth, their scars pressed together and they both felt how they pulsed, aching ever so slightly.

Karels's sense of smell never returned. And He did leave her, suddenly and unexpectedly. In the night. In His sleep.

JANA EGLE (1963) is a poet and writer. Her collection of stories, *Gaismā* [Into the Light], won the 2017 Latvian Literature Award. Egle also sees songwriting as a great part of the literary tradition, and actively participates in the bard movement in Latvia. Her story "The Quarry" was published in the February 2018 online issue of *Words Without Borders. Birthday* is her fourth book.

ULDIS BALODIS is a linguist, lecturer, and translator. He holds a PhD in linguistics and has a particular interest in endangered and lesser-spoken languages. His translations include Rūdolfs Blaumanis's *In the Shadows of Death* (Paper + Ink, 2018) and *Nakedness* by Zigmunds Skujiņs (Vagabond Voices, 2019), and contributions to *Trillium* (Livonian Culture Center & International Society of Livonian Friends, 2018)—the first-ever poetry anthology in English and Livonian, an endangered Finnic language native to Latvia.